Somebody Else's Sky

By Rob Durham

Edited by Greg Hardy

ISBN: 9798797199359

For Beth

I know that starting over's not what life's about
but my thoughts were so loud I couldn't hear my mouth.
—Isaac Brock, Modest Mouse

I know someday you'll have a beautiful life,
I know you'll be the star in somebody else's sky.
—Eddie Vedder, Pearl Jam

 1

Drew Brennan worried. Other than their brief pregnancy scare a few months ago, it wasn't like Kelly to be late. He paced from the living room to the kitchen and debated calling her a second time. They were supposed to leave for their tournament any minute.

As he laced his Pumas, he thought up possible reasons for his girlfriend's tardiness, ranking them from likely to unlikely.

Traffic – Friday in the northern Chicago suburbs. But why wouldn't she answer her phone? Her SUV had Bluetooth. If it was an important call, she wouldn't put a client on hold for him?

Work – As a mortgage broker, Midwest Bank's youngest at twenty-five, Kelly kept much longer hours than Drew. That's why every morning they drove separately to the same building.

She forgot tonight was the tournament – As the two youngest pickleball players at their fitness club, Drew shelled out a hundred bucks two months ago to enter them into the advanced, mixed-doubles division. Pickleball, or 'geriatric tennis' as their non-playing pals referred to it, was a hobby he and Kelly excelled in.

Infidelity – He tried to laugh off the idea. When would she cheat? During a twelve-hour workday? And with who? The barista at Starbucks with blue hair? Plus, they were living together in Kelly's condo—and someday he'd get her to change her name from Treader to Brennan. All their friends were getting married, so their turn was coming. Drew felt ready.

He dialed her number again.

"Hello! You've reached Kelly Treader of Midwest Bank Mortgage Division. I can't—"

He stabbed his phone's red button with his thumb and strode back into the kitchen. The microwave clock showed ten minutes past the time they'd arranged to leave. So much for warming up.

He opened the fridge for no reason and then closed it. His favorite photo stared back at him while the appliance hummed. The picture, curled and mildly faded with age, was from high school. Kelly wanted to take it down, but Drew insisted it would always be his favorite. It was their first date. Their parents did most of the arranging, and Drew happily escorted the only female college freshman to attend his senior prom. That night felt like a win for Drew. She wrapped her arms around him when they slow danced and didn't act aloof around his friends. At the end of the night, she accepted a peck on the cheek. Despite what Drew considered to be the perfect evening, it took him years to get a second date.

And no wonder with as skinny as he was back then. During college he toned himself from lanky to an athletic build. His hair style matured from a buzz cut to a more styled look that matched his scruff. Kelly loved messing with his brown hair now that it was a little longer. Friends at work who saw them together often joked about what beautiful hair their children would have some day.

Despite how the picture had faded, it still captured how Kelly's hair shined a lighter blonde back then, a little dyed. Now her thick hair, though still golden, held a more natural shade. And at five-foot-nine, she didn't just catch glances, she owned every room she entered. When she wore heels, she equaled Drew's six-foot stature. Depending on the outfit, she could portray effortlessly curvy like a pin-up or sleek like a runway model. Naturally, Drew noticed all the men who stared at Kelly. He always trusted her though. He had to or they never would have made it this long.

Returning to the living room, Drew's mind twisted further toward the negative. He stared out the front window as the April sun hid behind a cloud. Which would be worse, a car accident or another man? A vision of Kelly on a stretcher, but then another of her unzipping her dress in front of a stranger. He dropped to the couch, sure of his doom.

Pessimism came easily. An unexpected stroke stole Angela Treader, Kelly's mother, from them a week after their prom date. And while it delayed any romance between Drew and Kelly, in the months that followed he supported her better than any of her college friends. He provided a shoulder to cry on and an ear for listening, compared to her sorority sisters who relied on beer bongs and body shots to get through a weekend. One night on the phone, Kelly revealed her appreciation to Drew.

"I feel like you're the only one who cares about me," he heard her say between sobs. That's when he knew he won her heart. By the time she could smile about life again, Drew became a college boy alongside her at Northwestern and the relationship was a given.

Drew kept a picture from their first "real" date on his phone. A selfie at a Chicago Blackhawks hockey game with Kelly's arm wrapped tightly around him. The way Kelly looked at him in the photo helped him overcome any insecurities in the relationship.

He heard someone parking, but could tell almost immediately from the louder engine it was a neighbor's car and not Kelly's SUV. Everything about her candy-apple red MINI Countryman stood out as much as she did. As he grew more impatient, he let his phone distract him. Recently, he'd uploaded two YouTube videos from their previous pickleball tournaments. The numbers were blowing Drew's mind. In under two weeks, the clip of their championship indoor match near Milwaukee they won on New Year's Day totaled just under eighty-five thousand views.

Drew and Kelly dominated in their performance, striking a number of tricky shots. On one point, their opponent hit the ball at such a wide angle that Drew could only fire back an "around the post" forehand. The ball traveled past the side of the net, instead of over it, hovering a few inches above the ground for a winner. A few moments later, Kelly chased a deep shot down and while facing away from the entire court, struck the ball between her legs, sending it between the opponents who could only stare in disbelief. Kelly gave a playful curtsy to the cheering spectators before high-fiving Drew. Kelly also did the honors on championship point. She poached to Drew's side of the court and smashed a weak lob into the face of the male opponent. That afternoon, the pickleball gods were on their side.

Yes, there were grander professional tournaments online, but none of them featured Kelly in a short pink skirt and tight tank top. In the video's comments section, viewers promised Kelly representation if she wanted to seek out endorsements. Other comments offered her a new partner for mixed doubles. What if one of these commenters was a psycho who tracked her down and did who knows what to her?

Moments later, the front door swung open and Drew snapped free from his mental torture.

"Change of plans," Kelly announced, tossing her Michael Kors purse onto the couch. She returned to her phone call and began laughing with someone.

Drew held out his hands and then picked up their gym bags. "We're late."

Kelly raised a finger and returned back outside to her MINI, letting the cool spring air into their home. Confused and upset, Drew followed. Finally, she ended her call and opened the back of the vehicle. Had she stopped at the carwash?

"Sorry, don't be mad. I have something else for us tonight."

"But—"

"I know, I know. This is better. Besides, we're playing in that other tournament in a few weeks."

Drew thought of the nonrefundable hundred-dollar entry fee. That was nothing to Kelly, but with Drew's salary as the bank's customer service associate, it was a blow to his budget. He'd been depositing as much of his paycheck as he could into a savings account to buy her a ring.

The wind blew Kelly's hair into her face, and she paused. Drew brushed the strands aside, a habit he often did affectionately, and she continued explaining.

"What if I told you my dad got us tickets to a fundraiser at the Langhorn for tonight? It's for the Windows Coalition."

Drew tilted his head and sighed. He was probably supposed to know what that was.

"C'mon, Drew. It's fancy. Tickets were over two hundred bucks each. And …"

She reached in her trunk.

"… I bought a new gown."

Drew's mouth twisted. He loved formal occasions with Kelly. He followed her inside, carrying the dress wrapped in plastic.

"And," she held the word longer this time, "it's an open-bar event. I'll drive."

Drew softened and returned to his spot on the couch. "Will there be top-shelf bourbon?"

She was in the kitchen and didn't answer. Drew collected bourbons. He inherited a few bottles from his grandpa, and because some were of rare vintage he devoted time to learning the lingo.

He tried again in a friendlier tone. "Can you ask your dad if they'll have nice bourbons?"

Without turning around, she said, "For two hundred bucks, there better be."

Swanky fundraisers came with the territory of Kelly's job. More networking led to more money. In a gown, finding a conversation was never a challenge for Kelly Treader. Drew conceded because her salary paid for most of the mortgage on her condo. And the seascapes that decorated the walls. And the plush king-sized bed they shared. And just about everything else in their home because his college apartment decor was quietly disposed of when he moved in after his graduation. He would sulk a little, but it was no use starting an argument. He took off his tennis shoes and tossed them toward the front door.

"Are you still mad?" Kelly called from the kitchen. "I just texted dad and he said the bourbon will be on point."

"Your dad used the phrase 'on point'?"

"No, but … anyway, we don't have to leave for an hour and a half."

"Have you seen our YouTube numbers? We're becoming pickleball royalty," Drew called. But all he could hear was Kelly's heels clicking around in the kitchen. What was she doing in there?

"Our change of plans gives us a little extra time," she said. Without looking at him, Kelly strutted past wearing only her black Jimmy Choo heels.

Drew had forgiven her before she got to the stairs. They had the rest of their lives for other pickleball tournaments.

2

An hour into the fundraiser, Drew finished his second bourbon on the rocks. The crowd swelled through the brilliant hotel ballroom as Drew stuck a finger between his tie and neck. The conversations and the six-piece brass band grew louder.

It turned out the beneficiary of this night's event was a downtown homeless shelter. He recalled it was a favorite cause for Kelly's mom. Drew always tried to keep track of the roulette wheel of who the money for these swanky events was supposed to help. Usually it was for victims of a disease or natural disaster. Sometimes it was a school or scholarship fund. Every so often it would be for veterans. Whenever it was for the homeless, it somehow struck home closest to Drew to imagine where he would turn if his luck turned and he needed to bunk somewhere in a pinch.

Kelly had been schmoozing with an older couple looking to move from the city to the suburbs. Drew waited like a patient child. He lifted his drained glass and nodded at Kelly. She dipped a nearly empty martini glass and smiled. "Vodka," she mouthed.

Drew almost tripped on a woman's dress on his way to the bar. A lone bartender darted back and forth, mixing and pouring as best he could to generous cash tips. Drew realized he hadn't left anything his first few rounds when the crowd was lighter. Now everyone was stuffing cash into the jar. Drew would be waiting awhile.

He shifted and looked back at Kelly. Her blue gown had a noticeable but classy neckline, though technically nowhere near her neck. Two other men joined her conversation, and Drew caught their eyes stealing glances at her cleavage. One man nudged his buddy and pointed at his left hand. At first, Drew thought he was asking his wingman for the time, but then it hit him. They exchanged raised eyebrows because she wasn't wearing a ring.

Drew refocused on finding a gap in the crowd so he could get the bartender's attention. No openings appeared, but Kelly's father, Terry, joined him.

"Having fun?"

"I am Mr. Treader. Thank you for the tickets."

"What's with the 'Mr. Treader' nonsense? You haven't called me that since you got to college."

It was true. Once Drew and Kelly became an official couple, Drew grew more comfortable around her father.

Terry kept a friendly smile on a face only weathered by an abundance of tropical vacations. His hair was silver but thick. Dapper as usual, he greeted everyone with a righteously firm handshake. Among his successful businesses was the cleaning service where Drew's father was the general manager. Terry never flaunted his wealth, especially around Drew's folks when they often socialized, but Drew suspected the largesse not just trickled but streamed into Kelly's lifestyle. How else could she make down payments on her SUV and condo?

"Since we have a moment," Drew motioned to the crowd in line for cocktails, "I wanted to ask you something."

"Is it about your old man? Rick isn't going to retire on me, is he?"

Drew shook his head. "You know I've always loved your daughter. And I know I owe you big time for allowing us to live together, since my parents ..."

"Your parents are just old-fashioned, Drew. You have your father to thank, anyway. He's the one who promised me you'd always take care of Kelly. I trust his word as much as I trust him to keep my cleaning company's reputation spotless."

So far, so good. And the euphoria from the bourbon eased the words from Drew's mouth, but perhaps too quickly. "I want permission for your daughter—your daughter's hand ..."

This wasn't how he rehearsed it. Or had he rehearsed it at all?

11

"I want to marry Kelly."

Terry leaned back and gave a face like Robert De Niro's character in a mob movie after he just heard news about a heist that went sideways.

"Your folks and I always assumed you and Kelly would tie the knot. Are you sure you're ready?"

Drew felt his face burn like a bad shave. He was hoping for a congratulatory handshake and perhaps they'd hug it out. Maybe Terry's eyes would gloss up a bit. But they remained as focused as a sharpshooter.

"I'm very sure I want to marry your daughter."

Drew declared it louder than he meant to. A bald man over Terry's shoulder gave a surprised glance.

Terry's teeth shined with his smile. "I should've asked, 'Are you sure *she's* ready?'"

"Only one way for inquiring minds to find out."

Terry still hadn't given his blessing. He slipped between the shoulders of two men at the bar and looked back to Drew. "Are you sure she thinks *you're* ready?"

Drew took a moment to unfold the question. He really could use that third drink. Or had he finished three and was on his fourth?

"Gin and tonic," Terry said to the bartender over the cacophony. He turned back to Drew and pulled a ten dollar bill out of his wallet before sliding it onto the bar.

"She wants you to be a husband, a father … the man of the house." Terry shrugged. "A bigger house."

Drew struggled to find a comeback about his job and salary. "I'm only twenty-four."

Terry received his drink. "Exactly."

He flashed the apologetic smile of a shark that wanted you to know you could be its next dinner then strode away.

Stunned, Drew missed his chance to step up to the open spot at the bar. Had Terry already discussed this with his daughter? Drew and Kelly lived together happily, so marriage was the next logical step. It's not like Kelly was going to quit the pill and become a baby factory the moment they began their honeymoon. And if it was the other way around and Drew was the cash machine, Terry would go apeshit with his support. Kelly was wealthier because of her family. Her mother's life insurance probably paid for a lot of college. Then Drew remembered she had a full ride scholarship, so that policy could have paid for anything else.

Drew whirled around to locate his girlfriend. He saw that two more disillusioned suits had joined her circle.

He thought about the humble savings account he'd begun in college after his first real date with Kelly. It totaled just over two thousand dollars and was labeled on his statements as "The Ring Fund." Sometimes at work he would visit the account history and marvel at how he'd added a hundred dollars here or fifty there. Birthday checks, side jobs, whatever hustle he could find all went toward her engagement ring. He was so sure that his life would never be complete without her. His current total wasn't enough for the ring of her dreams yet, but it was a solid start. He could swing a payment plan for the rest. All he knew is that he was sick of strangers looking at Kelly's bare ring finger and acting as if they saw she sent a two a.m. "U up?" nude photo.

"Sorry," said a voice that snapped Drew back to reality. It was the bald man who had reacted to overhearing the ill-fated conversation. His drink was empty too. "Mikalis," he introduced himself. "Mikalis Andino."

His handshake was solid, but not in Terry's master of the universe vice grip. "If you just need a couple beers, they have coolers in the hallway."

"She doesn't drink beer," Drew said. "Plus, when there's top-shelf bourbon available …"

"I hear ya on that. I'm a connoisseur myself."

"I'll need something barrel proof after how that talk went," Drew said.

"This is probably none of my business, but just because she drops her panties for you at age twenty-four doesn't always mean she's the one. Have you not had any others lined up?"

"No. But believe me, she's the only girlfriend I've ever had and the only one I've ever even wanted."

"You're her only boyfriend?"

Drew wasn't. "We started dating in college at Northwestern. She's a year older, and our families are tight and—"

"If you've never been with anyone else, how do you know what's right and wrong in a relationship?"

"I'm telling you, I won the lottery."

"Show me the lottery winner who earned their jackpot and didn't blow it all away within a year."

Who was this jackass? Drew ached to change the subject. "Speaking of lotteries, have you ever hit up any of the local bourbon raffles?"

"I have," Mikalis said. "I own a restaurant called Ulysses. I pride my bar with a hell of a bourbon selection. You can mark anything up, and it's easy money."

Mikalis stepped toward an opening at the bar, but it closed quickly.

"We offer a few rare bottles. Technically, you could call them unicorns."

This was one of Drew's favorite topics. It was a go-to with strangers he was forced to sit with at weddings. Drew's tone changed.

"I've got one of the rarest bottles out there. My grandparents lived in Kentucky and my grandpa got so old he quit drinking. When he passed away, he left quite a few for me. A slap in the face to my dad, but grandson always trumps son-in-law."

Mikalis stared, unimpressed. "Let me guess. Pappy Van Winkle 23 year."

"Just the 10 year, but it's almost gone. Ever had Earlington Reserve?"

"I've heard of it," Mikalis said in a way that he was still humoring this young man who needed life advice.

"I've got an unopened bottle of Devil's Rare 18," Drew said.

Now he had Mikalis's attention.

"I could use one of those."

Drew grinned, knowing he had one more thing that other men would covet.

"Would you be interested in me taking it off your hands for the right price?"

Drew winced. "There's sentimental value."

"Bet you could pay for quite a few wedding expenses," Mikalis said.

Drew knew the bottle was valuable, especially amid the bourbon collecting boom. But he never thought to appraise the price. The bottle had been nestled in the back of his T-shirt drawer. Grandpa Henry would understand.

Mikalis handed Drew his business card.

"Think about it, kid," he said. "If you're going to wheel and deal with anyone about this, remember who wants you to live happily ever after."

As Drew pocketed the card, the most beautiful blonde in the room caught Mikalis's attention. She somehow parted the crowd with a soft "excuse me." Mikalis gazed in awe as Kelly leaned forward on the bar, her open back revealing the color of summer skin. The bartender immediately was at her service.

"Belvedere Martini and a Maker's 46 on the rocks," she ordered.

"Make it two Makers," Drew said. "One for my new friend."

The bartender's frown was countered by Kelly's smile. "Also, could I please have two olives in mine?" she asked. The bartender's grin returned. Kelly posed against the bar, tapping the toe of her right shoe against the floor. Her subtle flaunts always attracted wandering eyes.

Kelly handed a drink to Drew then one to Mikalis, who failed to find the words beyond his smile to introduce himself.

Pretending to be oblivious to the attention, Kelly turned to Drew. "Honey bear, you got the tip?"

Drew fumbled his last three wrinkled dollar bills onto the bar. Kelly raised her glass.

"I have to get back to what might be some new clients," she beamed.

Drew watched as Mikalis's gaze followed Kelly back to her circle.

Mikalis Andino took a big gulp of the bourbon then blinked hard. "Forget everything my stupid ass said. Marry her tomorrow."

"I would if I could."

"Sell me that bottle. You've got my card."

3

Kelly lingered in bed the following Monday morning, waking Drew up with her naked body pressed against him. This wasn't unheard of, but Drew let his mind consider what the occasion might be. Maybe she felt guilty for making them miss the pickleball tournament. It could be her potential clients at the fundraiser didn't pan out. Or perhaps her father had let the pickleball out of the bag about the marriage talk. Back and forth he weighed the possibilities, which helped himself last longer during the impromptu challenge of unscheduled workday morning sex. Kelly didn't mind the brevity. They had to hurry to the gym anyway.

The morning grew more memorable when Drew and Kelly were approached by two new pickleball opponents. A tall man with wide shoulders bounced a ball against the side of his paddle. He had dark hair with gray streaks and a bald spot, and a Middle Eastern complexion. Though he wore a permanent smile, his extravagant mustache and accent intimidated Drew more than a little.

"You kids play? I'm Bull, and this is my partner, Louisa."

A woman who was the size of an espresso shot to Bull's cafeteria urn of coffee waved hello with her paddle. She was clearly older than Drew and Kelly, but it was still possible she was Bull's daughter.

Drew and Kelly introduced themselves and took their spots on the far side of the court. Normally, they weren't vocal during these early morning matches. They let their play do the talking. Drew was about to warn Kelly, "This is going to be tough," but he could sense she was thinking the same.

Bull lined up his serve and called out, "Louisa is beginner. Don't hit all the balls just to her, okay?"

Drew rolled his eyes and nodded while Kelly mumbled something about playing just for fun.

"Zero, zero, start," Bull declared. He tossed the ball and hit one of the most unorthodox serves Drew had ever seen. Bull was a lefty, so the ball curved away from him before it landed. When it bounced, the ball jumped the opposite direction back at Drew. The shot jammed him, and he shanked his return into the net.

Bull laughed. "You like my serve? I call it Turkish Delight."

Kelly raised her eyebrows and smiled. She would have to field the next serve. Instead of any "Turkish Delight," Bull served a fastball that landed near the back line. Kelly barely adjusted and returned the serve a few feet in front of Bull. It bounced to his waist and hung perfectly for his forehand. He smashed the ball harder than Drew had ever seen anyone hit a forehand. Like a stray bazooka missile, it traveled head-high at Kelly, who somehow ducked by collapsing to the court.

"Juuust out," Kelly said. Her voice was playful, but her look was stern as Drew helped her to her feet.

Bull howled a laugh. "Oops. Almost took off your pretty head."

Kelly turned to Drew. "Let's beat the piss out of these two," she hissed.

Like so many times before in practice and in competition, Drew and Kelly fell into a rhythm of drop shots just over the net that caused their opponents to pop their shots up a little too high. Drew quickly got the hang of the Turkish Delight serve, along with a few other Bull originals, and they established a lead.

"Not very fair," Bull pouted, now that it was clear his partner was a liability. "Next game, we swap. I take your pretty wife, Louisa belongs to you."

"Sorry, we don't swap when we swing," Kelly said, locking her arm to Drew's. "This guy's my package deal."

As Drew wondered if Kelly meant the innuendos, she whispered their new strategy. "Hit everything to Bull the rest of the game. Keep his international competition ass on the bassline."

Drew smiled and obliged. Two points later, Kelly left one of her drop shots a little too high, which gave Bull a chance for an overhead smash. Drew absorbed a chest shot that stung like a paintball.

"My bad," Kelly said. She walked closer to Drew. "I'll make it feel better later, okay?"

Shell-shocked, Drew nodded. He took his time getting back into position while Bull aimed more trash talk. Kelly turned back to Drew.

"Seriously, if we can beat this guy I'll sooo make it worth your while tonight."

She winked and swung the seat of her desirable shorts toward Drew. He tried to keep his game face, but paused to blow a kiss.

"Time for my secret weapon," Bull crowed.

He rocketed the next serve at Drew, and the ball caught the sideline. Drew lunged and extended his paddle enough to make contact, returning the ball back to Bull. With Drew out of position, Bull's best shot was to simply hit it toward the void. Kelly realized this, waited, and then poached to Drew's area. Bull didn't see her coming and lofted a safe forehand. Kelly was in position plenty early and smashed back a shot that ricocheted off Bull's thick ankle.

Bull didn't say much as Kelly and Drew finished the final few points.

"Ahh, you pick on my partner too much," Bull said. The four met at the net to tap paddles. "Who plays singles? You or wife? I take you on. Either one."

Drew and Kelly exchanged a laugh. "I have to get to work early," Kelly said. Paddle in hand, she jogged off the court. Louisa walked away slowly in the same direction looking dejected.

Drew debated correcting Bull on how he described his marital status, then realized how proud he felt that anyone thought of Kelly as his bride.

"I don't really play singles. Sorry, Bull ol' buddy."

"Psh! I would not either if that was my partner. She pretty good. I mean, you're good too, but usually female partner is weakness."

"We've been playing together for years with our parents."

"And pretty. Very pretty. You must have lots of money." Bull laughed again. "My daughter should be so lucky."

Drew shrugged. He'd let this character out of *Game of Thrones* believe he was a prince too.

"I see you next time?"

"Hopefully," Drew said. They tapped paddles again and Drew left the court with a smile as wide as his pickleball paddle.

***

As always, Kelly arrived at work earlier than Drew. Her easily identifiable red MINI was perched in the first spot of the employee parking lot while his Civic, faded-blue featuring a white streak near the front bumper, squeezed in back by the dumpster. There were days when customers were already lined up at the door before he entered.

Drew didn't loathe his job, he just didn't do much while he was there. His duties were limited, and he never felt obligated to hunt for extra work. When he was first hired, his colleagues treated him with kindness and patience because he was Kelly's significant other. He handled the annoying customers who needed help balancing their account or opening a safe deposit box. He could notarize a title and relay interest rates, but if he called in sick, no one feared that the Dow Jones Industrial Average might tumble.

There was an art to looking busy. Drew mastered it by avoiding eye contact with the chattier tellers, and they in turn never asked for favors. More choreographed moves included every so often picking up his desk phone as though he was aiding a customer. Sometimes he'd bring up a spreadsheet on his computer, put the phone down, frown at the screen, then wait until his boss got sidetracked before he resumed browsing the web (always on his phone, so the IT department couldn't track his sites).

Craig Devlinger, the only personal banker and therefore head honcho of the branch, mostly tolerated Drew's minimal effort but occasionally asked more from his customer service associate.

"Guess what day it is," Craig said, approaching from his small office in the corner of the branch.

"Game two of the Blackhawks series?" Drew tapped the Blackhawks Bobblehead on his desk to spring it into motion.

"That and CD renewal day."

This sounded like real work.

"We need you to call all these boomers and get them to renew their CDs for another twenty-four months."

Craig dropped a folder of call sheets on Drew's desk like a bomb bay door opening in a black and white World War II movie. "Retention leads to bonuses."

"All of them? Today?"

Craig nodded.

Drew thumbed through the stack of accounts. It would certainly intrude on his two goals for the next few hours: Calculate how much he could get for the bottle of Devil's Rare 18 bourbon and find an engagement ring that wouldn't force him to sell his plasma. Or more likely, a kidney.

Craig recited a short list of instructions and then walked back to his office. "Be sure to stress the limited-time promo rate," he said before briskly shutting the door.

Drew smirked. It was rare that Craig handled anything with his door shut, but it would allow Drew to steamroll through his call sheets a lot faster. Once he reached four renewals he told himself it was a sufficient total and slid the chore aside.

Whenever Drew used his cell phone for internet access, he placed it just left of his keyboard. Occasionally he would pound on the clunky plastic keys while his left hand scrolled him down Reddit rabbit holes. Eventually, he found an essay about the bottle Mikalis Andino had on his most-wanted list.

Devil's Rare 18 was an accident spawned from an accident. According to the author, the distillery's warehouse was burnt to the ground from what was suspected to be insurance fraud. What appeared as a total loss actually yielded three somewhat intact barrels. One barrel was over-the-top smoky and its proof beyond drinkable. The second barrel was spared from the flames completely. It tasted terrible, and reputable experts agreed this was why they decided to burn down the warehouse in the first place. The third barrel, however, lodged itself into a perfect location and received just enough of the live flame to alter the blackened barrel's effect on the bourbon. The texture was smoother than anything on the market and tastier than even the fabled Van Winkle family of bourbons the rest of the world raved about. Since the barrel survived hell on earth during the fire, it was named Devil's Rare. The 18 represented the number of years before the barrel was opened and bottled.

Drew looked up from his computer. The story sounded like a myth, but then again, crazier things than that happen in Kentucky every morning before breakfast. Drew Googled more leads on the bottle through secondary markets. He clicked every bourbon website checking out their ridiculous price-gouging. Anything that listed Devil's Rare 18 followed it with N/A. At last he discovered a business with a price below a thumbnail photo of the familiar looking bottle.

The asking price was nine thousand five hundred dollars.

Drew wasn't just sitting on a unicorn. He was sitting on a unicorn with a monogrammed leather saddle who could fly from Kentucky to Lake Michigan in ten minutes because she just did three lines of cocaine.

When Craig emerged to check the progress, Drew pocketed his cell immediately and hoped his eyes weren't as wide as highball glasses anymore.

"Stats," Craig demanded.

"Four renewals, eleven retired postal workers had to think about it, five wives had to ask their husbands, and a St. Patrick's Day parade worth of voicemails."

Craig grinned, coldly but satisfied. "Keep at it," he encouraged as he exited the lobby jingling a keychain that would make a middle school janitor blush.

Drew could decompress when Craig disappeared like this. A two-hour lunch? Leaving at four to squeeze in nine holes before it got dark? Drew would slack just as much at his desk.

At lunchtime, Drew's fingers shook as he sent a text to Mikalis Andino asking for nine thousand dollars.

Within minutes, Mikalis replied.

"A bit high. I'll counter later on with what I think is fair."

It was enough for Drew to shift his research toward rings. He'd already familiarized himself with the basics of diamonds on the day two years ago when Kelly told him she loved him. He had surprised her with a "just because" Hallmark card in front of all of her friends causing a four-alarm swoon.

"$5K," Mikalis countered. Drew ignored it and returned to his online window shopping.

Drew continued to click on local jewelers, but his hand shook so much it was hard to control the mouse. At noon, he took the elevator to the third floor to visit the goddess who would be rewarded by all of his research.

The mortgage department contained a dozen or so cubicles for underwriters and other departments. Property management and accounts payable were foreign languages to Drew; he barely grasped what went on in his own assignments.

Kelly's incredible rookie year at Midwest Bank's mortgage division landed her a private office with a window. Drew poked his head in, and like most days, she was on the phone. Her office had three file cabinets, a white board calendar overflowing with appointments and notes, a wooden-framed photo of her mother, the bank's only reliable color printer and a desk with her laptop that had two computer monitors attached. She could've been mistaken for a CIA spy. All these files and forms made Drew's head hurt thinking about their complexity, but the office maintained an organized neatness. He marveled at her professional aura, which was as sexy as everything else she did.

"I'll need your wife's signature on both forms too," she said into her phone as she looked up and smiled at Drew. "It's on the back. Very important. Yep ..." She rolled her eyes in frustration with the caller then picked up the picture frame as she often did while stuck on the phone. One time she explained why she was so attached to the photo.

"My mother's image reminds me of who I can become."

Angela Treader went from a housewife who barely earned a dime her entire life to a certified home appraiser in less than two years. She was on the cusp of opening her own business when her life was cut short. Every time Kelly looked at the photo, the determination and ambition in her eyes nearly scared Drew. It was the same fierce look she sent opponents on the pickleball court. Drew also recognized this look when Kelly's father discussed anything about business with her.

Drew envied the relationship Kelly maintained with her father. Rick Brennan raised his son on the sports lore and statistics of the Cubs and Blackhawks, Terry Treader taught his daughter how to make a killing in the stock market. Drew learned how to start a lawnmower, Kelly learned how to take advantage of the prime interest rate. Rick counted down the days until he could retire and joked about working for "the man" while Terry elected not to retire even when he actually was "the man."

When the call ended, Drew saw her desk phone still blinked spastically with voicemail alerts.

"It's your lucky day," Kelly said. "I have a surprise."

"Already had my lucky morning, so—"

"Oh stop." She pulled two glossy Blackhawks tickets from an interoffice envelope. "They're for tonight."

"Where did you … How?"

"Just a little thank you from Regional Vice President Frederick Adams. He noticed my numbers last quarter. Two and a quarter closings a day." She obsessed about her average daily closings like a major leaguer with a batting average. If she didn't seal two deals per a day, she saw the hours as a failure.

"Congratulations." Drew picked up the tickets and smelled the shiny ink. Lower bowl seats at the United Center for a second-round playoff game were a dream.

"Here's the thing, though."

"No," Drew protested. "No thing."

"I can't go. Maybe take Devlinger? He helped with a few referrals this quarter."

Drew's shoulders dropped. "Can't you come with me? Even if we're late?"

"I have a closing at four and another at seven, and I have no idea how long they'll take."

Drew sat in the chair at the side of her office. He didn't want to watch a game with his boss. "You're the one who earned them."

"It's fine. As long as corporate acknowledges my numbers." She lifted the phone. "I'll call Dev now." She turned on the speakerphone as it rang.

"Craig Devlinger."

"Adams gave me Blackhawks tickets for tonight. I can't go, so Drew wanted me to see if you were up for it." She winked at Drew, who made a sour face.

"Tonight? Shit, my twins have some school program. One of them has to dress up as Ben Franklin and the other is Captain America. I can't."

"On a Monday?" Drew asked.

"Yeah, they don't ruin your weekend with these things. Just weeknights. You two will see someday."

"We'll find someone else," Kelly said. "I hope Ben Franklin and Captain America are on the same team at least and not fighting each other."

"Me too," Craig said. "Try Lee, maybe. See ya."

"Lee, are you still out there?" Kelly called.

Lee Jeffries, a Texan who migrated to Chicago long enough ago to embrace the Windy City but who still talked in Longhornisms, was the maintenance man for the area's branches. Drew had passed him near the elevator while Lee was atop a ladder fixing something in the ceiling. He lumbered into Kelly's office.

"Heard my name." Unlike the business attire of the rest of the staff, Lee sported work jeans and a Breaking Benjamin T-shirt. Quick-witted, Lee often led goofy, often inappropriate conversations when he wasn't tinkering with something. He loved introducing himself as the "Maintenance Acquaintance," which always made Drew roll his eyes. Lee was roughly thirty going on fifteen and usually seemed to be in the best mood of anyone in the building, even on days when the sweat glistened from his sun-scorched forehead to his jet-black goatee.

"You free tonight?" Kelly asked.

"I am," he nodded. He pointed timidly at Drew and whispered, "I reckon we should be more secretive so he ain't jealous."

Kelly smiled and Drew laughed as Lee slugged his shoulder. "Oh, you meant for the fella who barely works."

"Hey, I actually called a few dozen customers this morning," Drew said, faking a smile.

"What'd you call them? Idiots?"

Kelly sustained an amused grin. "Interested in seats for the Blackhawks tonight?"

"Hells yeah!"

"Great. Drew will pick you up."

Drew shot a look back at Kelly wondering why he had to drive. Then again, he couldn't complain about free tickets.

"Tell you what," Lee said. "Let me text you my buddy's address. I'll be over there helping him pack for a move. We can add a little pre-gaming too."

"And that's why you're driving," Kelly said to Drew.

Lee and Drew exchanged numbers.

"Is the house nearby at least?" Drew asked.

"Apartment. Ten minutes, tops," Lee said. "Thanks, Kelly. I need to get back to these air ducts, but I'll close the door so you two can have a quickie."

Lee laughed on his way out.

"What's wrong?" Kelly asked when she saw Drew's blank stare. "Lee's fun. And he does so much around here."

"Do you think Craig was lying?"

"Who cares? He didn't want to go, so his loss. Plus, you need male bonding other than your boss."

Practically all Drew's close college friends had left Illinois or moved to a distant side of the city. Most of his male interactions were with husbands of Kelly's friends. They were always older and wore pleated khakis and talked about European soccer and white wines. Or their kids. Maybe Lee would be fun.

Drew's phone chirped. It was a prompt from Mikalis Andino. "Counter offer?"

"$7500," Drew texted back. He wished there was an emoji from stepping on an ungrateful cheapskate restaurant owner's neck.

"Who's that?" Kelly asked.

"Maybe I have a surprise for you, too."

Kelly's cell phone rang. "Guess I'll have to wait and see."

While Kelly arranged a closing, Drew ate his lunch of turkey on white bread and pretzel sticks. Another text came back.

"Can't do $7500. I'll have to get back to you."

When Drew finished eating he waved to Kelly. She waved back. Her hand needs a ring, Drew thought as he headed downstairs. Vintage bottle of grandpa's bourbon, don't fail me now.

4

Drew had texted "HERE!" three times to no response before double-checking the address Lee texted and started pounding on the apartment door.

The door opened and Lee invited him in.

Drew didn't budge. "We should try and beat crowd—"

"No pregame brewski?"

Drew shook his head. "Too much traffic."

Lee sighed. "Fine. Let me say adios to my buddy."

Drew turned to indicate they should get to his car.

"He's leaving tomorrow. Military. Gone all summer."

Drew stepped inside behind Lee, who trounced up the steps to the apartment's second floor.

The apartment lighting was dim except for the TV, which aired a nature show. That's when Drew caught sight of a girl in the kitchen. Was she crying? She was perched on a chair, her shoulders narrow, and sobs were escaping her lips. He couldn't tell if she was a child until the scene on the television glared a snow-packed landscape. The brightness illuminated her body and he now sensed she was an attractive young woman. Her tiny shorts revealed toned legs that she hugged with slim arms. The TV glare darkened again, and Drew couldn't tell if she had turned to look at him.

Lee stampeded down the steps. "Let's roll."

Dazed, Drew expected Lee to acknowledge her. He didn't. Who was she? Something was ethereal and delicate about her.

Instead, Lee walked and babbled about which route to take to the United Center. Consumed by the girl's haunting image, Drew unlocked his car and opened the passenger side door.

"Are you serious?" Lee asked as Drew held it open for him. "You fixin' to put your arm around me at the game too?"

"Huh?"

"I don't require much chivalry." He chuckled as Drew realized what happened. "Man, you have to get out with the fellas more."

"Sorry. I was in la-la land. I have a lot going on."

"Well, I know it ain't work," Lee joked.

Drew shifted out of park and the trip began. If he was honest, he would've said he was right-click image-saving those legs to his memory bank, but guilt made him keep that to himself. What if that was Lee's buddy's teenage daughter? And if you're Kelly Treader's boyfriend, you do not mention looking at other women. Instead, Drew shared a different secret.

"I'm going to propose to Kelly. I'm selling an heirloom to buy her a ring and …"

Lee stuck out his lip and nodded. It reminded Drew of the face Terry made. Maybe Lee wasn't the ideal confidant for this subject. Drew's mind returned to the girl.

"So, your buddy is gone all summer? He have kids?"

"Nope. Divorced."

"You don't have any kids, right?" A last box to check before Drew could assure himself the mystery girl wasn't a child.

"I got snipped last year. No little ninos in my future."

Drew couldn't understand why a man would rule out having a family at such a young age.

Lee must have read Drew's silence. "Guess we're different on that front. It's okay, you can knock Kelly up."

Drew nodded as they reached a stoplight backed up with traffic. He pulled out his phone and texted Mikalis Andino. "7 is as low as I'll go."

***

Their seats were less than a dozen rows behind the home bench. The atmosphere was unlike any game Drew had attended because all he could ever afford were regular season tickets. He felt a sense of pride in his Blackhawks jersey. It was a black throwback style with his name "Brennan" above the number 1 on the back. When Kelly bought it for him on his birthday, he told her he'd buy one for her someday with the same name.

The game itself didn't yield much action other than occasional collisions against the boards. Instead of cheering, Drew was left to battle his curiosity about the girl. For whatever reason, he wouldn't let himself ask Lee about her. As the game wore on with no scoring by either team, Drew texted Kelly a few times but never received a reply.

During the second intermission, Drew tried to call her. The voicemail picked up before a single ring. Unusual.

He turned to Lee. "I tried to call her. You're my witness."

Lee rolled his eyes, then asked. "How did you two meet?"

"I was nine years old and at the company picnic for my dad's work. Kelly's dad owns the business, and my old man is the manager."

"This isn't the short version, I'm feeling."

Drew shrugged. "I love telling the story. We were playing hide and seek, and I crawled under a pine tree. She followed, and then—" The horn blew to signal the end of intermission. "She held my hand."

"And you've been together since?"

"Not quite. I went to Northwestern, too, and lost my virginity to her the summer before my junior year."

Lee lifted his fourth Miller Lite. "Dude, you're a trip."

Maybe it was the two beers Drew had downed, but he was ready to continue about how he waited outside her dorm in the rain with flowers, but those kinds of tales were for Kelly's friends, not the maintenance acquaintance from work.

With under five minutes left in regulation, Drew's phone buzzed. Kelly texted to tell him if everything was okay she was going to bed.

After a penalty was called on the Blackhawks, Drew told Lee, "I'll be right back," and scooted against the knees of the fans in his row. He exited to the concourse, where he had more privacy to call her.

"How's the game?" Kelly asked.

"No score. Everything good with your closing?"

"Ugh, I don't want to talk about it."

That's when the arena's horn blared and the crowd erupted in cheers. "Sounds like the Hawks finally found the net," Drew shouted.

"Great." Kelly seemed not as thrilled. "Gotta go. Love you."

"I love you too."

Kelly usually said "I love you," not just "love you." Had he done something wrong? Was it that she worked late while he enjoyed the perk she earned? She was the one who told him to go to the game.

It was easier to return to his seat because everyone in the arena was standing.

"Hope the call was important," Lee hollered over the ovation. "Biggest goal of the season and you missed it. Short-handed, even!"

"When you're in a relationship, you have to have priorities."

"Were you a priority to her earlier? Guess not, or she'd be here instead of me."

They spent the rest of the game and the ride home without saying much else to each other. When Drew pulled into the apartment's parking lot, Lee slurred a short, "Later, buddy," as he hopped out of the car. He went straight to his oversized truck and pulled out before Drew shifted out of park. He wondered about the girl inside. Was she alone now? Was she still crying? That's when his phone buzzed with a text.

It was from Mikalis Andino.

"$7k it is. Send me your work address."

Drew smiled and pulled out of his parking spot. He figured he'd never see that peculiar pixie again, and that was okay. He was set to buy a ring the size of a hockey puck if need be and next week propose to the love of his life

5

"No," Kelly said.

Drew paused before rising from his knee. Kelly rarely joked about serious matters, but she had to be this time. Suddenly, the candles he'd arranged and lit around the living room looked as ridiculous as he felt. Kelly strode into the kitchen and started boiling water on the stove.

Drew stared at the ring. He took it out of the box and twisted it with his fingers. A two-carat, princess-cut rock that cost him more than eight thousand dollars. Craig had steered him to a wholesale jeweler with a great reputation for helping the lovelorn who were shopping in his price range.

A tiny part of Drew, maybe his inner child, felt like crying. As the shock wore off, pain settled deeper than any emotional wound he'd ever felt. It dawned on him this was the first time he experienced true heartbreak. He'd spent all afternoon prepping for what was to be another legendary romantic anecdote, but now Kelly focused her attention on making macaroni and cheese.

Anger swelled as he walked into the kitchen, and it was all he could do to hide it. Kelly was reading the box as if she didn't know how to make one of her favorite comfort foods. Instead of looking up she said, "Babe, you know you're … we're not ready."

"Did your dad warn you I was going to ask?"

"No."

They stayed silent as Drew imagined that Kelly was now playing scenarios in her mind of how his talk with her father might have gone. After she set the noodles to simmer, she turned to talk.

"Drew, things aren't how they're supposed to be. You're barely making anything. How are we going to be able to afford a child? I'll need more than six weeks off, you know. Most of my income is commission and incentives."

"I asked you to marry me, not make a baby."

"This condo is okay for now, but I don't want to live here for the next decade."

"I don't make enough money to be worth marrying. Understood."

She held a wooden spoon in her ringless left hand. Her voice wasn't soft anymore. "You don't try at work. I bust my ass for eighty hours a week and you stare at the wall like a kid in detention."

Drew fought the instinct to cry. "My job is not as busy as yours. Sorry I'm not in the banking superstar hall of fame."

"You don't have to be a superstar. But ask anyone in that building who they think does the least on a day to day basis." She poured the steaming water down the drain and separated the noodles.

"Craig never says anything bad about me."

Kelly kept stirring the plain noodles. "You sure?"

"Fine. I'll ask him tomorrow. 'Hey Mr. Devlinger, I'm as bored as you're ugly. Please let me clean out the old safe deposit box files so my girlfriend will want to marry me.'"

"Play dumb all you want."

"And if I'm so poor and worthless, how did I afford a ring? Or is it not big enough?"

Kelly was silent until her eyes widened when it dawned on her.

"That bottle."

Drew had started to grin at her in respect to his ingenuity, but as she continued the grin flew away.

"You seriously sold an heirloom bottle of liquor to buy me a ring. That's what I'm worth. A bottle of booze you inherited."

Drew fumbled for words, but Kelly continued. "What about wedding expenses? Were you counting on pickleball prize money? I guess at least you would've earned that."

"Oh, like your rich father didn't help you with the down payment on this place. You magically had thousands of dollars straight out of college at your disposal?"

She dropped the wooden spoon into a bowl and turned off the stovetop. She left the kitchen and marched upstairs. Drew followed, preparing an apology.

"This is getting out of hand. All I want to do is make you my wife."

When she turned in the hallway to look at him, her face was bright red.

"Drew. I love you. But I hate you right now. For you to question how I provide a home that you live in for a fraction of what a real man would be able to afford is the most bullshit thing you've ever said."

He followed her into the bedroom. "Isn't the whole reason we're living together is because we're going to get married? Maybe I shouldn't be living here if that's not the plan."

"You still have a lot of growing up to do." She shook her head. "You don't think I don't want to get married? I'd love to put that ring on and plan a wedding. How many friends' weddings have we sat through? Yes, I want it to be my turn."

She isn't herself tonight, Drew thought. Could they just get past this? Part of him waited for her to say she was kidding and of course she would marry him. They'd pranked each other before.

That's when Kelly told him what he would later consider to be the ultimate gotcha.

"If you feel guilty about being unmarried and living together, move the fuck out."

***

Drew's second-biggest mistake that week was telling his mother he was proposing. Maryann Brennan yearned for a daughter-in-law and a church pew full of grandchildren.

She called him on his drive to work the next morning, and Drew didn't know what hurt more: his back from sleeping on the couch or his inability to sugarcoat his circumstances.

"Fix it!" she screamed.

"She said no. What am I supposed to do?"

"Don't you dare break up with that girl."

"I'm trying not to?"

"Andrew," she said, almost sobbing. "You and Kelly are destined to get married. We owe that to the Treader Family."

"Mom, we're not in some medieval aristocracy."

He heard her take a deep breath. "They've done so much for us."

"Dad had that job before Kelly and I dated."

"Your last two years of college ... Terry paid for most of that. Thousands of dollars. And then with you two living in the same home before ..."

"I did my part! Blame Kelly, not me."

"Your father is not going to be happy at all."

"I'll call him tomorrow."

"He's very tight with Terry, maybe let me talk to your father first."

Rick Brennan raised his son as best he could. With a working man's income and sixty-hour work weeks, father-son time was limited. He taught Drew how to shave, how often to change an air filter and the indignity of being a Cubs fan, but he dreamed of a better life for his only son. Once the Treader and Brennan families became tighter, Rick realized his son's potential. Kelly became the daughter his parents never had.

"He's not going to talk to me, is he?" Drew asked. "Mom?"

"You know how your father is, Andrew."

"Yes. Irish and uncommunicative."

"Have you talked to Kelly today?"

"Nope. I slept on the couch and heard her leave for the gym." Drew was thankful that it meant she would have gotten ready for work there and spared them the added awkward silence.

"Is she at work?"

Drew pulled into the last spot in employee parking. "She's not going to talk to me at work. Her car isn't even here yet."

"Where is she?"

"She drives all over the place for closings, Mom."

"Be sure to apologize."

"Apologize for proposing."

"For whatever you said afterward."

The call dropped as he opened the door to the bank. Or had she hung up on him? He didn't care.

Drew pocketed his phone, oblivious that all four tellers and Craig were staring at him. When he arrived at his desk there was a massive white cake with the words, "Congratulations Kelly and Drew!" in blue icing.

He shouldn't have told his mother … nor Craig.

"Sorry?" Craig offered as he scratched his thick neck.

Drew slumped in his chair. "I was surprised too."

Craig walked closer with his back to the tellers. "A couple beers after work maybe?"

His invitation was comforting. Drew's emotions swelled in his eyes and he nodded yes as Craig lifted away the cake to the breakroom.

The tellers gladly demolished the cake before eleven a.m., and luckily for Drew, lobby traffic was minimal. That afternoon, Craig mumbled something to the tellers and left an hour early claiming he had a meeting at another branch.

"I'll text you the address of the bar," he said with a wink.

After surviving the workday without encountering Kelly, Drew eagerly drove to the location Craig had sent. When he arrived, he hesitated to get out of his car. He was at Playoffs. It wasn't a strip club, but he knew stories of the suburban landmark's ill repute.

"Lee and I are near the bar," Craig had texted. "Enjoying the view!"

Other than the prevailing odor of grease, the first thing Drew noticed once he was inside was skin. Cleavage and abs and legs. Drew watched as girls weaved around with pitchers of cheap beer and heaping trays of fried bar food. The lighting gave off an odd, soft hue, but it could also have been that grease coated every inch of the air.

"Howdy. Just you?" said a blonde who might have just sprung to life from an eighties hair band music video. She put a fist on her hip and stuck out her elbow. "We'll make sure you don't get lonely."

"My buddies are over there," Drew said evenly. Craig waved. She walked him to the table anyway. He couldn't help but check her out from her head to the toes in her stripper heels after she handed him a laminated menu.

"She's looser than ashes in the prairie wind," Lee offered.

"Huh?"

Craig slapped his menu on the table. "Drew was picturing her naked and having wild fantasies on the pool tables. That's what this place is for."

"I was not!"

"Relax," Craig said as he poured the last of a pitcher into a pilsner glass.

The trio discussed the hockey playoffs until Drew noticed Craig looking at Lee as if they'd planned an intervention. "So you and Kelly are … on …"

Craig looked toward the ceiling for the right words.

"… a break?"'"

"No," Drew protested. "We had a fight, then I threatened to move out."

"Need a roommate?" Lee asked.

"I was bluffing." His bank colleagues exchanged a look. "What did she say?"

Craig grimaced. "She knows you're bluffing. And the tellers know you're bluffing. She was shitting on you in front of them while you were in the breakroom for lunch."

"Which tellers?"

"I'm not at liberty to say. But she's winning this fight."

"I didn't know you kept track. I didn't know there was a score." Drew gulped his pale ale. "I'll hold onto the ring until she's ready."

"You know what I did a few months before I got married?" Craig said.

Lee considered his empty mug. "You tried men?"

Craig laughed. "I broke up with her. She said she didn't want to live with me before we were married, so I dumped her ass."

Drew was intrigued. "For how long?"

"Maybe a week. The invitations had been mailed and everything. Women want to get married. I knew I'd get my way."

"Do you regret getting married?" Lee asked.

Craig waved at a waitress with jet black hair, who then darted next to him and he threw his arm around her waist above her gym shorts. Drew watched Craig's fingers squeeze her hip.

"I'm not following," Craig said.

Lee laughed. Craig laughed. Drew frowned and thought about the photo of Craig's family that hung in his office. His redheaded wife. His twin boys. If they could see the man of the house now.

"Who's the cute newbie?" the server asked as she broke free from Craig. She leaned so close to Drew he could smell her perfume, which smelled like everything in the Macy's makeup counter mixed together.

Drew introduced himself and held out his hand. She pushed it down and bearhugged him.

"We don't shake hands here, doll."

Drew blushed as he glanced at her nametag – and ample cleavage – to see she went by Jasmine. He shifted his weight, hoping she'd release the one arm still around him.

"Need another pitcher?"

"Yes, mammaries," Lee said.

"Menus? Wings?"

Drew's temperature rose. She tapped her manicured nails on his neck while Craig and Lee casually discussed their choices.

"Just fries. I still have dinner with the family," Craig said.

Lee scoffed. "Seafood sampler."

"What do you want, gorgeous?" She and her breasts were almost in his face. No other girl had ever been this close.

"Rings," Drew stammered before clarifying himself. "Onion rings. Please."

Jasmine wiggled to the kitchen without writing anything down.

"Single life ain't bad," Lee said. "You could bag her tonight, I bet."

"Why would I leave Kelly for a waitress?"

"You can either come crawling back or take control of the breakup," Craig advised.

"We're not broken up! I mentioned I should move out, but there's no way I'm doing that. I'd have to move back in with my parents and commute an hour each way." Drew realized he was pulling a napkin apart.

"What if I had a temporary pad for you?" Lee asked.

"I'm not sleeping on your couch."

"Not with me. I have a friend who needs a roommate. You wouldn't even have to sign a lease. It would be for four to six months, tops."

Drew shook his head. "We've had fights before. She just isn't ready to get married."

"Or engaged," Craig said.

"I can't believe—" Lee started, but Craig held up a hand.

"Drew, on behalf of the male species and as your boss, just hear Lee out on the apartment opening."

"Fine. Who's the complete stranger I should move in with? Where's he live?"

Lee grinned. "Remember my buddy's place where you picked me up?"

Drew nodded, still picking at his napkin.

"He's the one who left. His sister needs a roommate. Not just to help with rent and chores, but to keep creeps from stalking her."

Drew's heart raced thinking about the girl in the kitchen. Suddenly, his curiosity made this plan no longer seem implausible.

"At least consider it. It won't cost that much, and if you need to move back in with Kelly, no big deal."

Drew gulped his beer. His buzz and imagination bubbled inside. What would Kelly think? Would he even tell her where he was staying?

"Her brother is okay with some guy he doesn't know living with his sister?"

"Charlie? He's laid back. I'll just tell him what a dork you are. I think you'll get along with her, too. She works afternoons and nights. You'll barely cross paths."

Jasmine returned with their food. She set the plates down and asked Drew if he needed ketchup.

"Sure."

She grabbed a bottle from a different table and slowly squeezed it onto his plate. It was a tight spiral and came off extremely suggestive.

"Let me know if there's anything else you need, cutie. Silverware, another beer, a shoulder rub …"

Lee laughed. Drew shoved an onion ring into his mouth and shook his head.

"See? A dork," Lee told Craig. Jasmine giggled and walked to another table.

Craig turned to Lee. "You know he's only banged Kelly? No one else."

"I put up better numbers last week alone," Lee said.

Drew couldn't believe what he was hearing. "I'm sure they were all lookers."

Lee ignored him. "I'll message Charlie tonight and talk to Niki."

The name Niki fit for some reason. Like Drew already knew it ahead of time.

Craig looked at his phone. "Sorry fellas, I gotta run." He slapped a twenty on the table. "Finish my fries and for God's sake have Jasmine do that thing with the ketchup again."

Lee became quiet once it was him and Drew. That gave Drew time to think. Would a temporary move work? He'd pack a few outfits, his best bourbons, and the ring, of course. He'd stay just long enough for Kelly to cool off. It didn't need to sound like an ultimatum or a breakup.

"Can I see how the next few days go with Kelly?"

Lee shoved a potato skin into his mouth and nodded.

"Where does Niki work?"

Lee pointed to the table and grunted. "Here."

On his drive home, Drew's mind nearly split in half. How could he consider moving out? He'd be a moron to let Kelly go. They'd talk and work through it like every other couple. Then again, he would be living under the same roof as a Playoffs waitress named Niki. It made him feel a bit dirty – but he liked it. Did she run around her apartment in Playoffs garb? He couldn't bury his curiosity.

It was after nine o'clock when he opened the front door to Kelly's condo. The lights were off. Kelly would pretend to be asleep in bed, he guessed, ready to dodge the conflict another night. At least he wouldn't have to explain where he had been. After going upstairs and seeing the bedroom empty, Drew realized she must be out with friends too.

He could hear what would pass as their advice.

"Dump him!" "Find a man who makes six figures!" "You deserve better!"

Drew's head hit the pillow, and a painful thought crept into his mind. What if she was moving on? All Kelly had to do was sit at a bar and suitors would pay for her cocktails all night. He'd nearly been strip searched by a Playoffs waitress, what might happen to Kelly on her first night back among all the single ladies?

Another fear struck him. Did he smell like Jasmine's perfume? He jumped out of bed and grabbed a washcloth from the hall closet. He rubbed his neck with warm water until it was red. As he climbed back into bed, he knew there was no chance of sleep until Kelly was home safe, next to him.

The clock said 11:35 when he heard the front door open. Ten minutes later she took a shower. What was she washing off? She never showered that late. By the time she got into bed, Drew felt relieved, angry and jealous. He had to say something, but all that came out was, "Are you working out tomorrow morning?"

"I am," she said. It was so matter-of-fact he wondered if she'd rehearsed it. She rolled on her side facing away from him.

"Okay," Drew said. "Me too."

It was a start.

***

Bull and Louisa practiced service returns as Drew arrived at the courts.

"Where is that better half?" Bull called out.

"Finishing cardio," Drew said. "She'll be here soon."

After a few minutes, he walked back to the treadmill he saw Kelly jogging on when he arrived. She wasn't there, so he checked the stair machine she often used. After that, he found her usual spin bikes empty as well. He wondered how many people tracked him performing this ritual.

Drew tried not to look desperate, but he felt like a toddler who'd lost mommy in the store. He walked back to the front desk.

Through the wall of windows at the entrance, he watched the tail end of her red MINI pull away.

He'd left his pickleball paddle on the courts, and when he returned Bull was practicing a new serve. "Sorry, she had a work emergency," Drew said.

Bull shrugged. "A shame. Maybe we play singles?" He looked at Louisa, who seemed happy to be demoted.

Drew agreed and stood on the opposite side of the net. Singles pickleball was a lot more like tennis, involving mobility, running and quickness. Drew felt his youth would give him an advantage.

He was wrong. In a matter of minutes, Bull demolished the twenty-four-year-old by scores of 11-2 and 11-1.

"Guess it was all your wife last game," Bull laughed.

Drew leaned over, out of breath, sweat dripping on the blue surface, and he begged off Bull's offer of a third game.

Bull put his paddle in his bag. "Maybe you need her more than she need you, eh?"

6

Right before Drew's lunch break, Lee entered the lobby with a toolbox. He set it down on Drew's desk.

"Whoa. You okay, buddy?"

Drew nodded. He was tired of the question. Earlier, two customers in a row asked him about his scowl that he couldn't hide.

"If it helps, the Bensons are cool with everything."

"Bensons?"

"Niki and Charlie."

"Thanks, but like I said, I'll need a few days to think."

What Drew couldn't say was that the offer was tempting, he just didn't have the courage to accept it.

Lee shrugged then took his tools into Craig's office while Drew sulked. He rubbed the welt on his bicep where Bull had smashed a ball earlier. The holes from the ball left a pattern of circles.

Kelly could have told him she didn't want to play instead of just ditching him. And where was she last night until eleven-thirty? What else would she pull to humiliate him?

Drew decided he would at least let Kelly know how upset he was and that they needed to sit together later. Even if she couldn't talk much now, anything was better than passive-aggressive mind games.

He climbed the steps instead of using the elevator to calm some of his steam. He faked his smile through the cubicles of nodding acquaintances. As he neared her office, he realized he had no idea how to begin or how he would keep his emotions in check. He told himself he'd settle for an agreement to talk after work that night at an established time.

When he arrived at her door, he recalled how happy he was the last time he entered. Now his stomach was a knotted mess, and not just because he hadn't eaten all morning and hadn't packed a lunch.

Kelly's door was cracked. He could hear her on the phone, cheerful and using the friendly tone he hadn't heard in days. When it sounded like the phone call was wrapping up, he entered without knocking.

"Maybe three o'clock then?" she said into the receiver of her office phone. Drew was not acknowledged.

He stood silently, resisting the urge to sigh as her client call continued. Then Drew could tell their conversation changed to the client's children. And Kelly kept asking questions. She was testing his patience.

Drew leaned against the door frame. He watched the minute hand on the wall clock move six times until the call ended. Drew opened his mouth to speak, but she began dialing without taking the receiver from her ear.

"Are we doing happy hour later?" she chirped into the phone. Drew did his best to keep his jaw from dropping. Was she even talking to anyone or did she just want him to go away? Another minute passed and she still hadn't looked at him. Drew watched two more minutes tick by on her clock as she continued to laugh. The discussion moved to British comedies on Netflix. "You have got to watch *Derry Girls*. It is so, so funny." Her laughter was blatantly fake.

Drew's heart became a mad drum trying to escape his chest. Was their relationship a joke to her? He no longer recognized this insensitive witch who ignored him. Frustration took over from the pain, and when Kelly paused in the conversation he stepped forward.

"I'm moving out."

He spun and walked back through the row of cubicles. He kept his gaze straight forward not just to avoid eye contact with anyone, but to keep tears from making this a complete defeat.

***

"That's all you have?" Lee asked.

He and Drew stood in the parking lot of Kelly's condo. The day was warm, so Drew didn't wear a jacket over his work shirt. "Guess we didn't need your three-hundred horsepower." He patted the side of Lee's Dodge Ram. Dust covered his palm. "I can still buy you lunch for your trouble."

"Forget it," Lee said. "You've been through enough."

Drew slammed his trunk shut. His possessions fit easily. He'd emptied his section of their closet and the drawers on his side of the dresser. There was a box of books, most of them classics he'd yet to crack, his bottles of bourbons, a telescope he hadn't touched since college, and the diamond ring worth more than everything combined. Drew kept the ring in his pocket. He ran in one last time and grabbed an extra set of sheets and towels in the hopes Kelly wouldn't notice their absence.

"I won't need a bed there?" Drew asked.

"Comes with the place. And she's got dishes and all that kitchen stuff." Lee looked back at the condo. "Your woman owns everything in there?"

"Just about. I couldn't find my lucky Northwestern cup though." It was a souvenir from the first college football game they attended as a couple. Even though the Wildcats lost, Drew scored by losing his virginity that night at age 21.

"Guess I'll head back to the bank," Lee said. "Craig's cool with you blowing off the afternoon?"

"I guess I'm his favorite down-on-his-luck employee."

Lee tossed Drew the key to his new residence and drove away in his dirty pickup.

Remorse teased Drew as he looked at the condo. He could unpack his car and give it another chance with

Kelly. Then again, Craig didn't give him the afternoon off for Drew to pull a bluff. He couldn't just let Kelly stomp all over his dignity. Moving out was only temporary.

He tried to guess her reaction after he told her he was moving out. Did she call her friends? Did she call her father? If so, Drew's parents would be informed within minutes. He checked his phone but hadn't missed any calls. He hoped Kelly hurt as bad as he did. Did she close her door and cry? Cancel meetings? Would she try to find him tonight or would she try and move on?

He recalled the day the two moved in together and how his mother fussed. But once everything was in its right place and his folks went home, Kelly and Drew spent the evening christening every room. It didn't seem like that long ago.

He debated making one last round through the home. The search for his missing cup was a legitimate excuse.

No, it was time to meet his new roommate.

7

As Drew pulled out the key to open his new front door for the first time, he wondered if he was supposed to knock first.

Lee assured Drew that Niki would be at work, but Drew still felt like an intruder. He noticed the faded, red doormat with the word "Welcome" barely visible. Kelly would've replaced it for a fresh one long ago.

He turned the key and slowly opened the door. The lights were off and things looked different from his last visit. His eyes shot to the kitchen where he'd first spotted Niki. There was no one there, of course.

After hauling in a few boxes, he found a light switch and began inspecting the downstairs. The television looked to be forty-eight inches and had a newer feel than the furniture. The couch and recliner showed years of wear and tear. There was none of the feminine decor of Kelly's home. Even though the downstairs was much smaller than Kelly's condo, the vanity ceiling gave the illusion of volume.

In the kitchen were two wooden chairs and a table with a *Vogue* magazine. The counter was empty except for a toaster, an empty bagel wrapper, and a box of Life cereal. He opened the cupboards and saw an orphanage of mismatched plates, bowls, and glasses. He laughed knowing how appalled Kelly would be at the collection. His lucky cup would've fit right in along the U.S. Army and Playoffs assortment.

A Budweiser magnet held an April calendar on the fridge. Drew guessed that the starred days were when Niki worked. There was one on that day's date.

Lee had explained that Drew's bedroom was at the end of the upstairs hallway on the left. "The empty one. Not the one with the girly stuff."

Once upstairs, he saw Niki's door to his right. It was cracked open an inch. Down the hall on the left was his room, where a mattress and dresser were all that remained. This was the first time Drew had his own room since high school.

He hauled his remaining possessions upstairs in a half-dozen trips. Each time he passed Niki's bedroom, he fought the temptation to peek inside.

He set about making his bed by untangling the faded blue sheets he swiped. They smelled like Kelly. A day ago he wouldn't have noticed, but now that he was under a different roof, everything was different. He laughed, realizing he spread king-sized sheets on a full-size mattress. At least he'd have plenty of coverage.

He found his bathroom pleasantly clean. A lemon scent lingered over the spotless toilet. It was a relief he wouldn't have to share a bathroom with Niki. After peeing, he put the seat down out of habit before he caught himself.

"This can stay up from now on," he said.

He proudly raised the seat before flushing.

"This can stay up!"

Drew put the finishing touches on his room and found a home for the ring. He opened the box and perched it atop the dresser as a reminder of why all this was happening. They needed time to cool off, and eventually Kelly would wear the ring for the rest of her life.

The afternoon sun leaked through the open blinds. Drew wondered what Kelly would think about arriving to an empty home, and remorse tugged at his heart. He had time to return everything back to the way it was. He still had a condo key.

Drew's stomach growled. Groceries were next on his checklist, but the nearest store was still the same Meijer he always shopped. What if he ran into Kelly outside of work? He pictured her in the produce section exchanging numbers with another man.

Drew walked back down the hallway past Niki's cracked open door. He imagined he could learn a few things about her from a glance around the room. It was almost four p.m. and he figured Niki was either at work or elsewhere. He knocked on her door with one knuckle, and it opened a bit wider. He could see enough of her bed. Queen-sized with a tangled mess of lavender sheets and blankets. Completely unmade, which made him smile about how Kelly would view that. A pink T-shirt was draped over a small office chair by a desk that had a tablet propped up.

"Hello?" came a tiny voice behind him.

Drew jumped. At the top of the steps stood Niki. She was just over five feet tall and wore pink pajamas. Her short hair framed a face that seemed large compared to the width of her shoulders, which reminded Drew of every local TV news anchor. Her soft brown eyes held an innocence that might make a man want to take care of her more than himself.

"Drew, is it?" She held a full cereal bowl with both hands, so a handshake wasn't offered.

"I thought I heard you in here, so I knocked and …" He stared deeper into her stunning eyes.

She didn't say anything as she spooned the cereal into her mouth in the hallway.

"Yes! I'm Drew. I appreciate you letting me crash here. Lee gave me the details about—"

"Take a breath, sugar." She laughed, revealing sharp cheekbones. She wasn't wearing makeup and Drew noticed the faded freckles on her nose.

She and Kelly were opposite builds. For starters, Niki's chest was minimal but still contoured in the V-neck of her tight pajama top.

Drew realized Niki already knew she charmed him. For years he'd watched Kelly melt any stranger to get whatever she needed. Table for two? She'd touch an arm. Even women were wooed because they wanted Kelly to like them. Now Drew found himself swooning in front of a girl who wasn't wearing makeup or a bra.

A sliver of skin peaked out above her waist with a tiny hip bone on each side. Her pelvis was a paradox of narrow but shapely. Along with this doll-like figure, her natural tan complimented every shade of light brown.

"I know what you're going to ask," she said to fill the awkward silence. "I'm a quarter Cherokee."

"I—"

"Relax, Roomie, it's your home now too." She moved past him toward his room. "Are you unpacked? I would've helped but I was catching up on sleep. Late night last night."

She inspected his living space while Drew gawked at her from a new angle. Even her feet were adorable, and Drew wasn't one of those foot guys.

"Oh my gosh!" Niki put her cereal bowl on the floor and plucked the ring from its box. "What's this?"

"The reason I'm here."

"She said no to this?"

"I'm proud of the ring, just not the result."

Niki slipped the ring onto her finger and inspected the diamond as if it had magically materialized from beneath her knuckle.

"I need a mirror. Be right back." She ran out of the room. "I love it!" she called down the hallway.

Drew sat on his bed until she returned.

"I should get ready for work." She tried to pull off the ring. "Uh oh."

"Very funny. Nice try."

"No, seriously. It's stuck." She squinted in pain from the next attempt. "Darn it. I'm sorry."

Drew smiled at her. "You don't cuss, do you?"

"My fingers swell when I'm stressed out. I'll get it off eventually. A little help?"

Drew stood closer to her as she extended her hand. Not now, he told his racing heart. She held out her hand as if he was going to read her palm. Her nails were a natural color instead of the bright red of Kelly's expensive weekly manicures. The ring didn't move as he tried to twist it loose. He pulled again harder.

"Ow!" Niki jerked her hand back and inspected her finger.

"I didn't mean to hurt you," Drew said.

She didn't acknowledge his apology. "I have to go to work."

"But it's kind of valuable. Extremely valuable. Used car valuable."

"It's not going anywhere."

"Promise you won't wash any dishes or—"

"I've worn fancy jewelry before. We're fine." She turned and exited. Drew stared at the dirty cereal bowl on the floor.

What had he done thinking it was the right choice to move out? There had to be a way to salvage his life with Kelly. Maybe once they were married they could look back and laugh, but he knew his decision was an enormous mistake which explained the constant pit in his stomach. Much like the time they rolled the dice when he ran out of condoms on a road trip.

Perhaps he could forgive her first because of all of the work pressure she faced. He had to get life back to normal. The last few days she wasn't acting like herself. She never treated him so poorly.

He could sneak everything back to her home tomorrow. He could gaslight what he said in the office. "I said I'm moving out for a night or two. You were too busy on the phone to listen."

If he swallowed his pride, he could be back in Kelly's bed by their usual ten o'clock bedtime that night. A sense of relief with that plan loosened the tension in his shoulders. He scrambled and began gathering his clothes. It would be messy, but Kelly wouldn't kick him out for bluffing. They were a team. He remembered the YouTube video. It now registered at over one hundred and seventy thousand views, but he was afraid to read the comments.

While he watched the video, his phone buzzed. A text from Kelly.

"I need my key back."

For the second time that day, he shoved all his clothes back into the dresser. He set aside a handful of purple and white Northwestern T-shirts and even a pair for mesh shorts. Those would serve as the pillow he forgot to pack from the condo.

8

The next evening, Drew sat in his bedroom like a felon in prison. All day at work, he didn't attempt any interaction with Kelly other than texting that he dropped his key off in her work mailbox. She didn't reply.

The living room still didn't feel like a place he could call home. After a microwaved ziti dinner at the kitchen table, he retired to his room and practiced pickleball by smacking a foam ball against the wall over and over.

When he heard the door open downstairs, he set his paddle down and picked up a book titled *Proof: The Science of Booze*. Everything about bourbon fascinated him. He flipped the pages before a shame washed over him. Niki controlled his actions from the moment she arrived home.

Niki was so light of foot she could ascend the stairs without a creak from beneath the carpet. He heard her bedroom door close. With his door cracked, he listened from his bed.

Nothing.

He was about to put the book down when he heard a knock. She must float like an angel.

"Come in."

Niki was back in her pajamas from the day before.

"It's still here," she said, extending her hand. The ring sparkled. "I'm being careful."

Drew shrugged. "I'm sure it'll slip off soon."

"I got asked a million times about it. Plus, it killed my tips. All my regulars think I'm off the market."

"Does that mean you're on the market?"

She raised her eyebrows before changing the subject. "Are you using T-shirts for a pillow?"

"I meant to buy one today. But I was tired after work."

"You're tired because you didn't sleep well last night because you don't have a pillow."

She disappeared into the hallway and returned to toss a spare, limp pillow at him.

"Do you have a pillow case for it?"

Something about the gesture touched him. He nodded yes.

She turned to leave but then said, "Oh, Charlie wants to meet you. We're going to video chat in a bit. I'll holler when it's set up."

Drew fell back and tested the pillow. A bit thin but much better than his shirts. It gave off a hint of a scent, perhaps it was sandalwood. He put his pillowcase on it and now it smelled like Kelly.

"Drew, you ready?" Niki called.

Tentative, Drew walked into her room. The same sandalwood smell was present. Niki sat cross-legged on her bed and nodded at the chair. When Drew sat, he was met by Charlie's face on the tablet.

"Thanks for letting me stay in your old room," Drew began.

After a small delay, Charlie twisted his mouth. He looked about Lee's age and had a shaved head. Instead of Niki's slender fawn-like neck, Charlie's was short and thick, just like all the soldiers in the movies.

"You can thank Lee, I guess." He already sounded mad.

"Everything okay over there?" Drew asked.

"If it was, I wouldn't be here."

"Charlie Benson," Niki said in a motherly tone. "Why are you being mean?"

Charlie turned away and then back to the screen. His nostrils flared as he exhaled.

"Lee told me this guy was a big dork, and he's clearly … You're in my little sister's bedroom while I'm halfway around the world. Pardon the fuck out of me as I get used to that, okay?"

Drew looked to Niki for help. She smiled and nodded at him to get up so she could face her brother.

"I haven't confirmed he's not a big dork," she said. "And if I let him have his way with me in my bedroom, I don't think I'd livestream it to my big brother halfway around the world."

Drew felt a thrill shoot through his chest that this was her version of standing up for him.

"Maybe you can cheer Drew up instead of acting like a tough guy," she continued. "He's so heartbroken about his ex-fiancée."

Drew corrected her. "Technically, she said no to my proposal, so she never attained fiancée status to become an ex-fiancée."

"That's a million times worse!" Niki and Charlie said in unison with the same wide eyes of disbelief. Niki jumped off the bed to disappear downstairs, but Charlie kept looking through the screen.

"I'll be nice," Charlie conceded. "Drew, tell me what happened."

Drew filled Charlie in on the beginning, middle and abrupt end to his relationship. "But I'll get her back somehow," he concluded.

Charlie rested a hand on his chin. "She's banging someone else."

Drew cringed. "No, that's not it. She doesn't have time. She averages over two mortgage closings seven days a week."

"Did she have time to fuck you?"

"Yes."

"Now she has time to bang around with someone else."

Drew shut his eyes for a second. "If she …wanted someone else, why wouldn't she dump me? Tell me why you think she's cheating."

"Happened to me when I was married. She blamed it on my military tours, but I found out she was just as unfaithful when I was home."

Drew elected not to argue with a wounded man. He let Charlie vent about his very brief marriage and how he pictured himself living happily ever after with a couple kids instead of being a bachelor again.

"Let me give you some advice, Drew. You know what women find most attractive at your age?"

"Sky-high stacks of cash?"

"Ambition. Ask your boss what you can do to get promoted. Go above and beyond until he sees you as a threat. Nobody likes to be outdone by someone inferior in rank. They'd rather promote them somewhere else to get them out of their unit."

That's when Niki returned. "Okay, fellas. I was going to try and sleep tonight. Or should I crash on my own couch?"

"Don't let her sleep on the couch," Charlie said. "Always hurts her back."

Drew stood up. His legs were stiff. Niki stood behind the chair and rested her hands on it.

"What the hell is that on your finger?" Charlie yelled.

"Good night," Drew said and fled the bedroom as Niki calmed her brother.

Back in his room, Drew tried to call his father. He didn't answer.

9

"I want to make more money here," Drew told Craig first thing Monday morning. He'd rehearsed a handful of stronger opening lines, but that's how it came out.

Craig pounded away at his keyboard. "Customer service has a low ceiling. You're almost to it."

"Then make me a banker."

Craig looked offended as Drew sat in the chair across from him.

"Train me to be a banker, I mean. Please."

Craig rolled his chair a few feet backwards.

"Train you? Like I don't have other responsibilities here?"

"How did you learn the ropes?"

Craig smiled. He pointed through the door to the shelf over Drew's desk. "See those binders?"

It was the first time Drew noticed them.

"Take one home. Read it. Learn it. Repeat before moving to the next one."

"Can I shadow you too?"

"Shadowing is for Applebee's servers. We try not to creep out customers with an extra set of eyes staring at their bottom lines. We don't need them thinking there are people here who don't know everything. I want customers to trust that I'm the man."

Craig softened his tone. "What's all this about?"

"I'm trying to … you know, better myself."

Craig laughed knowingly. "I thought you would've moved on with that hot little thing Lee set you up with."

Drew imagined Charlie was there to shove a fist down Craig's throat.

Craig closed his laptop. "How's it going with her anyway? If she's like those other hot pieces of ass at Playoffs—"

"She's not."

A thoughtful look crossed Craig's face and he quietly mused, "If she's the one I think she is, her chest and back are interchangeable. No tits at all."

Drew didn't have a response ready from the script he had been preparing for this talk.

"A far cry from Kelly's legs that go on forever," Craig said. "You'll never land a piece like her again. There's always the memories, I suppose."

Drew rose and stormed over to retrieve the first binder. It covered his palms with dust. He read through it until lunch, which he now ate in his car. When he returned, Craig was at the entrance.

"Don't go in," Craig said. "Follow me."

His boss led Drew to the front of the building. A landscaper poured mulch near the drive-thru ATM.

"Look down the road. What do you see?"

Drew shielded the sun from his eyes. They felt tired from all the reading that morning. "Cars, businesses, light poles. That plaza with The Cheesecake Factory that mysteriously closed, and that stupid inflatable string bean balloon guy that flails around."

"A used-car dealership. There are a ton more as we get closer to the city, are there not?"

Drew nodded, relieved his boss's tone wasn't condescending anymore.

"I'm running a plan by Adams."

Drew tilted his head.

"Frederick Adams. The VP. Visits the branch a few times a year. I let him cheat when we golf together. Gave you the hockey tickets?"

"I've talked with him before," Drew lied.

"I'm going to work on these dealerships for high-risk, high-interest loans. As many as I can get. Dozens even. What'll happen is they'll sell cars to low-lifes with shit credit and it'll all go through us. But, they have to get a checking account, savings, and about five other products you'll learn about once you understand all those manuals."

It sounded like a great idea. "How do I help?"

"Learn the basics of opening accounts and closing loans."

Drew blinked while he processed the plan.

"While you're in study hall, I'll be out here wooing these sleaze ball dealerships and setting up the logistics. If we can pull this off, our branch will be number one in the company for loans, accounts opened and sales per new customer."

"What sales?"

Craig put his hands over his face as they returned inside. "Debit cards, savings accounts, overdraft protection, payment protection, blowjob insurance—"

"What?"

"Seeing if you're paying attention. There's also checking accounts, check books, and so on."

"How many people still use checkbooks?" Drew wondered.

"If they decline the checkbook, you order it delivered straight to the branch. We dispose of it, still get the sale, and the customer doesn't get charged a thing." Craig stopped to check a message on his phone. He grinned at what he read, then scowled when he turned back to Drew.

"You really haven't done much here, have you?"

"I'm ready to change that."

***

Drew awoke very early the next morning. He'd fallen asleep at almost one while studying his bank manuals but was in his workout clothes to head to the gym by five thirty. As he cleaned his oatmeal bowl, he heard the front door open.

"I missed curfew," Niki said. "Please don't ground me."

Niki unzipped her dazzling white boots from under the pant legs of her jeans and unbuttoned her creamy pink jacket. "My evening went a little long."

"That's none of my—"

"I fell asleep over there."

"I didn't know you had a boyfriend."

"We're friends. I have to tell him that about a hundred times an hour, though."

She walked past Drew into the kitchen. He smelled a touch of vanilla perfume. Drew watched her down a glass of tap water. Her makeup was heavier than usual, making her look older and sexier.

"Why are you up?"

"Heading into the gym." He picked up his pickleball paddle. "I like to get a few games in before work." He waited for her to inquire about his hobby.

Instead, she asked, "Why are guys so stupid?" He noticed her voice wavered slightly.

Drew shrugged. "Sometimes we misjudge a situation and—"

"I've known this dude since high school and nothing has ever happened between us. Why would he think tonight was the night?"

"What do you think made last night different?"

She peeled off her jacket and revealed a light blue cami that showed her shoulders. Drew felt an incredible urge to rub them. Slowly, she walked back into the living room.

"My brother is gone." She leaped face down onto the couch.

"Did they know each other?"

She nodded then yawned. "Can you cover me up?"

Drew spotted a gray blanket folded in the corner by the TV. He brought it over to her and paused, taking in the tiny but toned muscles around her shoulder. Carrying trays must be a good workout, he thought as he let the blanket unfold over her. His thumb brushed her arm and she shivered from the contact.

"My brother almost killed an ex-boyfriend of mine in high school," Niki said with her eyes shut.

"Oh yeah? What for?"

"He broke my heart. It was my first love."

Drew realized high school was much more recent for Niki. He set his bag down and sat at the end of the couch by Niki's bare ankles and feet. He pulled the blanket over them which triggered a smile.

"My boyfriend got really jealous of my guy friends and tried to tell me I couldn't hang out with them. Then he told me I couldn't wait tables because customers hit on me."

There was silence, but it didn't feel awkward. Drew wanted to skip his workout and curl up beside her.

"Charlie basically dumped him for me by saying that if he ever talked to me again he'd kill him." She wiggled beneath the blanket. "He doesn't like it when boys make me cry."

"I wouldn't either," Drew said. If he lingered any longer she would catch on. "Didn't Charlie say not to let you sleep on the couch because of your back?"

"He's not here to carry me upstairs."

Drew froze. It sounded like a test. He would've loved to cradle her and lie her down in her bed.

With her eyes still shut, she smiled and whispered, "Goodnight."

Drew stared a few moments and then headed to the gym. Bull destroyed him in three straight games.

"I'd say you should get more sleep in the morning instead of playing me," Bull said as they parted. "But you seemed asleep through the whole session. Keep coming in for our morning games, I enjoy your funny footwork."

Nothing phased Drew the rest of the day. Not when Craig badgered him about how many manuals he had left. Not when Kelly appeared behind the teller line for a brief consultation with a client. He didn't even worry about what Bull meant by "funny footwork." He kept his thoughts on Niki and how he wished he could've touched her more that morning.

When Drew got home from work, Niki was in the kitchen putting away dishes. He spotted a half-empty bottle of red wine on the floor.

"You off tonight?" he asked.

"I am. I'm going to try and pick up more day shifts during the week. I can make just as much if I work double shifts on the weekend."

Drew pictured sleazy customers throwing dollar bills at her like she was on a stripper pole, with Craig cheering her on and tossing twenties.

"Is your back sore?"

"A little." She turned and stretched her arms high. Instead of a tramp stamp on her lower back, she had two symmetrical dimples. Venus holes, Drew believed they were called.

She picked up the wine bottle and took a sip.

"Want some? I wasn't using a glass, so if you're worried about cooties."

Drew laughed and accepted the bottle. "No worries. I did want to ask you—"

His phone buzzed. It was his mother. He declined the call.

"Has my boss, Craig, ever hung out with Lee at your workplace?"

"Probably. Lee's always in there with a buddy or two."

"Craig's married."

Niki laughed. "Most of my biggest tippers are. And they aren't there because it's a happy marriage."

"Then why would they get married in the first place?" Drew glanced at the engagement ring stuck on Niki's finger. His phone buzzed again.

"Sorry, I better get this."

He was halfway up the steps when he answered.

"I'm in your neighborhood," his mom said. "Tell me where you live."

"Hello to you too. Mom, it's not a good—"

"Tell me where you live, enough of the shit."

He'd never heard his mother swear at him. "Mom, what's wrong?"

"Can't I pop in and see my son?"

"Can we meet for dinner instead?" He realized he'd lowered his voice even though he was alone in his room. "I haven't straightened things up around here."

"Oh, so she doesn't clean either?"

"Mom, what are you talking about?"

"You're living with a girl, right?"

"Yes."

"When I visited you at your home before, the place was always tidy. You never had a problem when I stopped by on a whim." Every few weeks he could count on his mother for dinner at a restaurant or a delivered home-cooked meal. "Is it so wrong I miss you?"

"It isn't a good day."

"Fine. I'll throw out this lasagna I spent all day—"

"Mom!"

"Let me pull over and give it to a homeless guy. Maybe he won't assault me."

"You can come over, but you can't—"

"I can't what?"

He wasn't sure. He just knew he didn't want her interacting with a roommate who had spent the afternoon drinking straight out of a wine bottle. "My roommate is having friends over, so—"

Drew turned around and saw Niki in the hallway, arms folded, the bottle dangling from the hand that bore an engagement ring intended for Kelly. He muted the phone.

"Trust me, you don't want to deal with her."

Niki let her lower lip pout. He put the phone back to his ear. His mother was rambling angrily.

"Please," Niki said. "I want to meet her."

His mom continued. "What are you hiding? Can't I at least meet the person you're living with? I'm not some crazy old lady who wants to cause problems."

Drew muted the phone again and looked at Niki.

"I'll be good," Niki said. She pulled her lower lip down with her thumb, rather suggestively. Then she mouthed. "I promise."

Drew widened his eyes at the bottle. She playfully hid it behind her back.

"Fine, but I'm not texting my address until we straighten up."

"Oh," she said. It must have been the word "we" that surprised her. "I'll see you soon."

After he hung up, Niki extended the wine bottle toward him. When he reached for it, she pulled it back and began to chug.

"No!" he said. She ran into her room, but he followed her to the door wondering if it was okay to intrude.

"Text your mom our address, Drew."

He obeyed.

"You better share that," he said. A game of keep away ensued. Like children, he chased her around her room, unsure of the boundaries. He'd played this game with Kelly a million times and it inevitably ended up with him pinning her on the bed. Niki knew what she was doing. Finally they froze, out of breath. Niki was on her knees on the center of her bed, straddling a pillow. Drew breathed heavily, gawking at her pose.

"You've got wine all over your mouth," he said. When she smiled, he added, "And your teeth are purple."

"I better shower and sober up," she said. "Here. Finish this."

Drew accepted the bottle and took a swig. It was warm and sweet. Niki got off her bed and walked into her bathroom.

"Want me to hide up here until after dinner?"

Drew couldn't tell if she was drunk, so everything in play was risky. Then again, if word got back to Kelly that Niki was a knockout, would that serve a better purpose? He would have to trust Niki.

Drew heard her shower turn on. "Well?" Niki popped her head out of her bathroom. Her shoulders were bare and Drew realized she was probably naked.

"My mom's not that scary. And I'm sure she made enough lasagna for ten people." His heart fluttered as he headed downstairs.

Maryann Brennan arrived carrying a foil-covered dish.

"I had to walk clear across the lot. Don't they have assigned parking for each spot like your other place? And are you going to show me where to set this so I can hug you?" Maryann fought her gray hair rather well and wore it longer than most women her age. Her eyes darted around.

"Get it all out, mom," Drew said. She could vent all she wanted while it was just the two of them. "What's on your mind?"

"It's so much ... cozier I guess is the nice way to put it."

Drew led her into the kitchen. "Thanks for bringing dinner. I don't eat much in the kitchen, but I cleared off the table."

"Mrs. Brennan?" Niki was behind them in the living room.

"Is that her?" his mom whispered.

"I think she found us." Drew whispered loudly back.

"Why are we whispering?" Niki asked as she entered the kitchen. Her hair was still wet and she wasn't wearing makeup. The freckles on her nose looked like tiny sprinkles.

Maryann looked Niki up and down. "Aren't you a petite little thing?"

"Hi Mrs. Brennan, I'm Niki Benson."

"You can call her Maryann." His mother shot a look at her son and then shook Niki's hand.

"Welcome to our home," Niki said. She went into server mode and set the table in seconds. "Would you like some wine?"

"Of course not. I drove here, and it's a weeknight."

"I don't drink during the week either," Niki said. "Maybe if I'm off the next day, but it just slows me down, you know?"

Maryann nodded at Drew. "I don't want to know how often this one is drinking during the week. Andrew and his bourbons."

"Who, me?" Drew laughed. "I've been working so hard, I don't have time to relax."

"I'll just have a diet soda," Maryann said.

Niki scanned inside the fridge. "I hate to say it, but I think this two-liter is flat."

"This is why we need more than fifteen minutes to get ready, Mom," Drew said. He enjoyed saying the word "we."

"Water is fine. Is that what you normally drink?" She spread her napkin on her lap. Niki filled a glass and two plastic cups.

"When we're out of bathtub gin," Drew said.

Maryann ignored the joke. "Where are you going to school, young lady?"

"No school. Maybe someday."

"Maybe? If you don't want to work weekends the rest of your life, you almost have to have a degree these days."

"Mom, please." Drew cut up the steaming lasagna and placed a piece on each plate.

"What? I was just asking."

Niki spoke up. "I look at Drew and how his degree is in ... what exactly?"

"Communications," Maryann said, shutting her eyes.

"Yet he works at a bank. It just feels like the degrees people get rarely fit their job."

"Where do you work now?"

Drew was about to take his first bite of lasagna but paused. "She's a server."

"You must make good money," Maryann said. "Professional waitressing isn't a bad gig in your twenties. Is it fine dining?"

"Only the finest," Niki said.

Drew lifted his fork. "How's Dad doing?"

She grimaced at her son, suggesting the man was still very upset. "He's a bit worn out. Working from home more. Says he's too old to hop around to every building like he used to."

Drew turned to Niki. "My dad manages a cleaning company. They clean office buildings and small businesses." He nodded at her left hand, and she quickly dropped it below the table.

"Drew didn't inherit the cleaning genes," Maryann said.

Niki laughed. "This is really good lasagna. I haven't had homemade food in forever. I get the Stouffer's when it's on sale."

"It's not an easy recipe," Maryann said. "My mother's side of the family was mostly Italian, so I learned from the best." She smiled, and Drew wondered if his mother was finally warming to Niki's charm.

"Niki, what do your parents do?"

It was something Drew wondered too but had never asked. Niki squirmed and took another bite. She nodded her head then sipped some water. "Mom hasn't been in the picture since I was a kid. She cheated on my dad."

"Oh, I'm sorry. What does your father do?"

"I don't know." She said it as if she was asked what was the square root of a million. Maryann gave Drew an alarmed look.

"She was living with her brother," Drew said. "He's in the Army, but he's overseas for, what, six months or so?"

Niki nodded.

"I'm sorry, dear. Where did you say you waited tables? Maybe Rick and I will stop by." She smiled and poked at her food.

"Mom, are you sure you don't want any wine?" Drew asked. "I think I'll have a glass. Italian food almost begs for it, right?"

"I work at Playoffs," Niki said. "It's a sports bar and grill, so probably not a romantic place for date night."

Maryann set her fork down and looked to the corner of the room like she was trying to remember something.

"Wait, is that the place that ..." She looked as if there was a fly in her food.

Drew quickly swallowed. "I'm having my boss train me to become a banker now, Mom. I have to study a bunch of manuals and then we have this plan to bring in high-interest loans."

Maryann kept her eyes on Niki. "You don't wear those skimpy outfits I see in the ads in the coupon section, do you?"

Niki bit her lower lip. "Push-up bra and all. Lord knows I need it."

"Oh dear," Maryann said.

Drew dropped his fork. It skipped off the table and onto the floor.

"I'll get it," Niki said. She got up and took way too many paper towels to the floor.

"I'm going to excuse myself so you two have some time to catch up," she said. "I'm feeling … not good."

Drew tried to look apologetic, but she hid her face. She wiped the floor and then abandoned dinner.

"Was it something I said?" Maryann asked. "And who is she engaged to? That ring!"

Drew was fully aware how sound traveled upstairs very easily.

"Mom, you sound judgmental. Who cares what she does for a living?"

"I was making conversation. I didn't say anything negative."

Drew found a new fork, and then his mother broke the silence.

"I guess Kelly doesn't have anything to worry about. That pixie won't steal you away with a microwave oven."

"That's why you're here, isn't it?"

"I thought you and Kelly were mending things. Don't you two have another picklebat tournament soon?"

"Pickleball, Mom. Pickle. Ball."

"You're still partners?"

"I doubt it. And you're just here to compare her to Kelly. You know we're not a couple."

"I should say not. She has no plans for school and works at an off-Broadway Hooters."

"If I moved in with a guy, you'd care what he did for a living? I think she's doing great for not having any parents in the picture. She makes more money than me, what's the problem?"

"I'm not stupid, Drew. She's a very attractive young lady. You're not attracted to her?"

Drew reminded himself that this conversation wasn't as private as his mother assumed. "Yes, she's beautiful. I'm aware."

"Well, she's definitely not Kelly. Don't you get distracted from your goal."

"My goal?" Drew wiped his face with a napkin. "Or yours?"

Maryann stood and started cleaning the table. "My grandkids."

After his mother left, Drew debated whether he should apologize to Niki. If she was already asleep, he didn't want to wake her. Then again, he didn't want to go the rest of the week without seeing her and letting her animosity boil up.

When he got to her bedroom door, he could hear soft music playing. A glow of candles shed light from under her door. He thought about knocking. He tapped on the door with his fingertips.

"Yes?"

"I'm sorry. She's just … like that for some reason."

"Come in," she said.

Relieved, Drew opened the door. She was in her bed, propped up reading a book. Drew sat at the desk and let his eyes adjust to the darkness. How was she able to see anything?

"What are you reading?"

"*Rebecca*, by Daphne du Maurier?"

"It looks hefty."

"Heavier than a guilt trip from a nosey mother."

"Sorry about her. Please don't think I'm judgmental too."

"You were this morning."

"I …"

"You were what?" There was a playful tone in her voice. "Maybe not judgmental but jealous?"

Drew fumbled for words until her sing-songy voice let him off the hook.

"You were jealous for sure, because I can stay out all night and you have to go to work."

"That's technically envy, not jealousy."

She set her book down.

"Envy," Drew explained, "is when you have something someone else wants. Jealousy is when someone has something that you consider to be yours."

Niki fiddled with the ring. When she blinked, her eyes opened very slowly. "Thanks for the mansplaining. Would Kelly be envious or jealous that I'm wearing her ring?"

"Neither. She didn't want it."

Niki pulled her knees to her chin and hugged them. She had survived his mother and he felt closer. She must have felt it too. For a moment he forgot about Kelly, and the pit that lived in his stomach since the breakup faded.

"What about when I was out with my friend all night? Envy or jealousy?" Her eyebrows raised suggestively. Then she turned away, inspecting the ring as if she'd just put it on.

Drew's mouth opened but nothing came out. Be careful and stick with the original plan, he told himself. Win Kelly back. Re-start your life.

Niki's phone buzzed next to her. "It's Charlie. He wants to video chat."

"Cool."

"You didn't answer." Niki fiddled with the ring.

He was not going to share his feelings with a woman whose family sounds like it was one crazy uncle away from starring in a reality series on a deep-discount cable channel. His father would disown him. His mom would kill him with one of her ravioli makers.

"Envy," Drew said. "Like I said, you're free to—"

She pulled off the ring and tossed it at him. It bounced off his chest to the floor. "I'll let you know if Charlie wants to talk."

Drew set the ring back in its box on his dresser. The way she suddenly pulled the ring off—how did that happen?

He lugged one of the bank manuals to his bed, prepared to master car loans. Once he got that down, Craig could leave him on his own at the branch. Drew tried to focus but kept second-guessing his answer to Niki. Admitting jealousy was his chance to tell her he wanted her. He looked back at the ring. The open box served as a reminder that he couldn't let himself fall any further for her and lose control of his life to another girl. Maybe it was only a mild infatuation. Kelly was the reason he had his nose in these manuals every night. Learn, work harder, get promoted, win Kelly back. After ten minutes, Drew realized he hadn't even opened the binder. When he finally did, Niki was in the hallway.

"Charlie's ready to talk."

He obeyed and walked to her room. The lights were on now and the candles had been blown out. A smoky scent lingered with a touch of vanilla.

Drew and Charlie chatted about the Cubs until Charlie asked, "Did she tell you what next week is?"

Drew looked at his roommate. She was reading her novel and didn't look up. "My birthday."

"Her twenty-first," Charlie said.

"That's a fun one," Drew said.

"He doesn't want to go out with my friends," Niki said. "Do you?"

"I haven't been out in a while, and my friends are all, well, not on my side. So, yeah."

Charlie laughed. "I lost a lot of 'friends' in my divorce."

Niki looked up. "You would go out with me and my friends?"

"Sure."

"I was hoping you could help keep an eye on her," Charlie said. "Some of her work friends aren't chaperones I can trust."

Niki rolled her eyes. "Tomorrow?" Drew asked.

"Next Friday after my shift."

"I can make sure things don't get too crazy," Drew said.

A night out with Niki and a gaggle of hot waitresses? Drew prayed their crew would run into Kelly.

Charlie nodded. "Sorry I was a little intense last time."

"You miss me!" Niki sang. "Say it."

She squeezed her way onto the chair next to Drew and her warm skin brushed his arm. Drew kept his arm firm, soaking in the contact. She focused on her brother and seemed oblivious to the touch.

"I miss you a little."

Reluctantly, Drew pulled his arm away and was about to stand up. "I need to get back to studying."

"That reminds me," Charlie said. "You do boat loans? I have a buddy who wants to buy a boat."

"I'll learn how to tonight. Does he know where our branch is?"

"Lee can tell him."

"I'd be happy to help," Drew said. He stood and gave Charlie a salute, wondering if he executed it properly. The feeling of Niki's arm left a warmth as he walked back to his room.

Sleep failed to come right away. The thin strip of light that invaded from the window was enough for his eyes to see the ring on top of the dresser.

After some time, he got up and closed the box.

10

Drew set a goal for himself Monday morning: focus on anything but women.

It didn't help during pickleball. Bull dominated him so badly he had time to lose four games.

Drew continued to fight any feelings toward Niki. What kind of a long-term relationship would he have with her while random creeps supported her through tips based on how far their imaginations took them?

Kelly made sense. The familiarity with her family was important. Not to mention it would get his mother off his back and his father would speak to him again.

As Drew parked at work, he felt he was failing his goal. "Starting now," he told himself. "Only work. No more worrying." After his pep talk, he slapped his steering wheel and exited his car.

When he entered the branch, he could feel all the eyes of the tellers. It reminded him of the cake day. What happened? Did they know if Kelly was already dating someone else? The pit in his stomach returned.

On his walk to his desk, he saw it. Spread across the far wall was a banner with Kelly's face, airbrushed to perfection, with the slogan: "Let Kelly Treader help you land the home of your dreams!"

Craig appeared from his office. "Marketing went a little extreme. Looks good, right?"

"I'd walk up and kiss it, but the tellers would start to talk."

Drew returned the manuals he'd borrowed back to their shelf and sat at his desk doing his best not to look at the banner. Craig remained in the center of the lobby, like he was waiting for another response from Drew. Instead, he threw Craig a curveball.

"I'm ready to close a loan today."

"You learned how?"

Drew recited the procedures and all of the products he'd attempt to tack on with the loan.

Craig nodded his approval. "The most important part is right after you finalize everything, you put it in my number." He paused. "Are you writing this down? Seven, nine, zero. Tattoo it on your forehead if you have to. If anything comes back on the loan, it comes back to me since you're not a banker."

Drew wrote it on a Post-It and stuck it to his monitor. "Got it."

"And it helps with my bonuses."

"How do those work?"

"It's a combination of loan totals, accounts opened, customer retention, new customers, and ..." He clicked his fingers. What am I forgetting?"

Drew shrugged. Bonuses were as foreign as choosing rum over bourbon.

"Vacation days! If I don't take them, I get paid a little extra."

Drew couldn't recall Craig ever taking a day off. "That must be lucrative."

"With you able to handle things, maybe I can finally travel somewhere." Craig stared into space as if he was envisioning his private place. Drew hoped it wasn't Niki's table at Playoffs.

Kelly entered the lobby from behind the teller line. She stomped a heel at the sight of the banner. "Dear God, my forehead is enormous."

"Craig told me he approved the whole layout personally," Drew heard himself saying while stifling a grin.

So this was how their first interaction would go after not talking for so long? They'd pretend nothing happened like divorced parents in front of the children. Drew read a confused look on Craig's face and then watched Kelly. She was as beautiful as ever. She wore black slacks and a black and red top. Her blonde hair was a little lighter and longer, like how she wore it in college. She kept her gaze on the banner as she neared Drew's desk.

"Craig's going to let me close a loan today."

"That's what I heard."

No you haven't, thought Drew. Could she be surprised just once?

She tapped two fingers on his desk before they made eye contact. "We're still registered for that tournament on Saturday, you know. The one back home."

Back home was near her father's house and not too far from his parents' home. "Have you been playing at all?" Drew asked.

"Dad and I played Sunday afternoon before cracking open one of his new bourbons. As usual, he's got something for me in the works."

"Let's play the tournament then."

Kelly smiled, though it seemed superficial. "Might as well."

She tapped his desk twice again. "Don't let the banner distract you too much," she said. "It's a picture, not a centerfold."

They both laughed.

"Bye, Craig," she said.

"Later," Craig replied and then approached Drew. "Looks like you former lovebirds could be friends at least."

Drew couldn't hide his smile.

"Clear it out of your mind because I've got a loan for you to close in a half-hour."

***

For the first time in days, Drew felt ... good? Stable?

As the week continued, he realized that the role of a banker wasn't all that difficult. Craig could have spared him the bulk of the studying and just shown him the basic procedures in a few afternoons. Instead, the manuals taught him even the abnormal loans like secured, unsecured, open-ended, and other bullshit jargon he overheard Craig use on the phone.

Craig began leaving the branch for hours at a time almost daily. This put them both in a better mood and took a lot of pressure off Drew. By Friday, Drew found himself enjoying his work and the interactions it entailed. He started to feel grownup and professional. Oddly, Craig's wardrobe had grown more casual. Sweaters instead of suits, khakis instead of dress pants. Maybe it helps with the car dealers, Drew assumed.

Lately, Drew felt like his business attire was no longer a costume he was forced to wear as a professional. Each morning when he looked at himself in the mirror, he found himself hoping he would cross paths with Niki on his way out. Unfortunately, her hours didn't mesh with his.

He bought a few new ties, spent a little more on his haircut, and shaved daily instead of every two or three days. His handshake became firmer. The old men who popped into Craig's office to exchange anecdotes began chatting with Drew. It turned out they knew a thing or two about fine bourbons and what was wrong with the call-up replacements in the Cubs infield.

Another motivation for Drew was the upcoming night out with Niki and her friends. On Friday, the anticipation made the final hours of work drag. On top of that, she never gave Drew a set time for when they would leave. He felt ridiculous sitting on the couch ready to roll during the six o'clock news while she was still at work.

Then he watched the entire Cubs game without so much as a text.

Was Niki's enthusiasm only a front for Charlie? Was he supposed to lie to her brother on her behalf? If something did happen to her and Drew wasn't there, Charlie would still fly back and wring Drew's neck.

Drew wondered if he'd been stood up. The sick feeling reminded him of the last night he had to wait on Kelly to come home. Maybe Niki was with someone. He scolded himself for becoming so smitten. He wasn't ready to move on. Being stood up wasn't even a scab to tear off, he was still bleeding from Kelly's breakup.

Maybe he should forget trying to have a relationship. He untucked his shirt and flopped on the couch. He'd heard of people who were so heartbroken that they stopped putting themselves out there. His heart grew sicker as eleven o'clock approached.

Then the front door opened. Niki entered wearing sweats that covered her Playoffs uniform.

"Give me twenty minutes," she said and scampered up the steps.

"No hurry," Drew said. He went out and tidied up his Civic. There was a chance he'd have to drive everyone home, so the gym socks and pickleball gear would have to move to the trunk.

Was this a date? Technically, he was taking her out with her friends. But they were meeting them there, and it's not like these girls were all going to be single. He would treat it like a date. Kelly remained the goal, but in the meantime and for the first time in his life, he was going on a date with someone not named Kelly Treader. If he found out that Kelly was testing the waters, he had this to comfort himself.

Drew knew he wanted Niki, but only on a superficial level. Just curiosity for what it would feel like to kiss someone else. He could handle it, especially sober. The sober person is always in control, he reminded himself as he returned to the couch for more baseball highlights.

An engine rumbled outside.

"Is Lee here yet?" Niki called down. "I'm almost ready!"

It was not a date if Lee was tagging along, Drew decided.

Lee pounded on the door and opened it before Drew could get up.

"Cubs win?"

"Only if you only count the first seven innings."

Lee lingered over the threshold and lit a smoke. Drew waved a hand as a cloud floated inside.

"Okay!" Niki said. She glided down the steps completely transformed.

Her eye makeup had a sparkly coral blue that made her face look like an angel's. She wore a black jumpsuit with a neckline that dipped below her belly button. The inner curve of her breasts, small but defined, peeked out.

She turned her feet sideways in her platform heels, cautious not to stumble.

"I say Go'dam!" Lee blurted. Then he whistled and clapped.

"Don't swear," she said.

When she got to the last step, Drew stood nearby and their eyes were on the same level for the first time. Something in his heart shifted.

"Do you mind?" She batted her eyelashes at him. They were false, but attractive.

"What are you asking?"

"I won't lose it." She held up her hand. The ring, of course. "And if any creeps try to dance with me ..."

"It's your birthday party, so how could I tell you no to anything?"

Lee stepped in and took her hand. "Then let's not waste any more time. My carriage awaits. Rusted muffler and all."

Drew bit his lip and watched Lee escort her to the large, black truck. A "Re-Elect W. For President!" sticker adorned the bumper.

"Drew, you are hereby relieved of designated driver duties," Lee said as he gunned the engine.

Drew nodded. "Sobriety and control are overrated."

11

Drew resented the ten dollar cover charge. The club was anything but crowded. Lee paid for himself and Niki in cash while Drew had to be taken aside to run his credit card. His friends didn't seem to notice he got stuck behind. After getting his hand stamped, he joined them at a large high-top table where three girls and two dudes were already drinking.

The ladies were clearly coworkers of Niki. Their outfits sported open backs and shoulder tattoos, and their makeup had more layers than the nachos supreme platter at Playoffs. Even their fingernails gave a "bad girl" vibe.

The guys looked scuzzier. Drew guessed they spent their discretionary income on roadside fireworks, Fireball Whiskey, and overpriced baseball caps that don't match the team's colors. They didn't bother to introduce themselves, though it was impossible to hear because of the pounding dance music. Instead they each put an arm around one of the girls.

"The hot ones are ours," they seemed to suggest, "and you can have the leftover."

Niki introduced "the leftover" to Drew as one of her best friends. He didn't catch her name but she somehow looked familiar. She slid her stool right up to his.

She sucked on a colorful vape pen and looked close to thirty. Her eyebrows seemed to be painted over her skin's natural dark complexion by one of those brushes used on a Thanksgiving turkey.

She offered Drew her hand. "Jasmine O'Keeffe," she purred. When she let go, her thumb lingered and rubbed the top of his fingers.

The Players waitress who did the ketchup thing! Drew now remembered. She looked different with her hair down. He wondered if she recognized him.

"It's a pleasure, Jasmine O'Keeffe," Drew said

"I know, I don't look like your basic Celtic lass. I'm part Filipino, Indian, and Columbian."

"Is there a term for that?"

She raised her eyebrows and took a big sip through her straw. "Exotic."

"The exotic Jasmine O'Keeffe."

"It's my ex-husband's last name. Asshole doesn't bother with alimony. Plus, O'Keeffe's meaning is far from accurate too."

"Why?"

"It means … gentle." She stared straight into Drew's eyes.

The music grew louder as Drew's brain scrambled to keep the conversation going. The best he could do was "I'm sorry the marriage didn't work out."

Lee swooped in with his knuckles contorted around too many shot glasses. "Time to get my group round of shots out of the way," he said, setting down eight purple glasses on the high-top table in front of Niki. "Bottoms up, birthday girl."

They cheered and downed the concoctions. A chilled, citrus-tasting sourness sank to Drew's stomach. Jasmine immediately perked up about an incident at work. Niki and the others chimed in, mentioning names Drew didn't know.

Several drinks into the night, the club grew crowded and bodies pushed into their once isolated tables. It was well after midnight, and conversation became even more difficult to hear as the music endlessly blasted. The two couples disappeared onto the jammed dance floor. Lee grabbed Niki's wrist and led her out as well.

Drew looked helplessly at the sea of strangers. Was this his life without Kelly now?

Jasmine smiled at Drew. He decided he might as well vent to his new admirer, even if the conversation was more yelling at the top of his lungs than pillow talk.

"The ratio of guys to girls here is so out of whack, it's a wonder our table hasn't been asked to join a fantasy football league."

"That means there are lots of guys here to buy me drinks. But none are as cute as you."

"How does anyone know these songs? The baselines are garbage and the auto-tuning makes me want to take shots of hard liquor through my ears.

"You don't dance?"

"Only at weddings when I have to."

She blinked and stared at him. "Wait. Did we hook up once?"

"You waited on me at Playoffs. With Lee and my boss."

"You smell good. Like candle store good."

This girl wasn't just flirting for tips at Playoffs, she really wanted him.

No one had hit on him in years. Without Kelly around, there was no longer a shield of blonde hair.

"Oh, just some cologne I found when I was moving," he said, hoping she would ask about it. Then he could talk about Kelly.

Instead, Jasmine leaned over and smelled his neck. Her nose slid along his skin sending tingles through him.

"It's working on me," she said. Her mouth was so close to his ear. Drew took a large gulp of his rum and Coke. "This isn't your scene, is it?" She tilted her head just like his mother used to do when he didn't answer right away.

"I feel very old."

She leaned back. "Well if you're old, Sweetie, how you think I feel?" They both laughed.

"It's Niki's birthday, so I figured why not celebrate it with her," he said.

Now Jasmine was the one tipping her cup back. She put a hand on Drew's.

"I'm good for another drink or two. When you're ready to get out of here, let me know."

She got up and strutted to the ladies' room. Drew noticed how short her skirt was. Was this the dating scene now? A few drinks, a buzzed drive to a strange apartment, then sex with someone you didn't know anything about?

"Mom, Dad, this is Jasmine," he thought. "She's probably thirty and makes tips because of a push-up bra. Oh, and she might have a kid from her first marriage."

He shook the idea out of his head as Jasmine returned.

She stood close to him instead of sitting. "Still hate this music?"

"I've heard car crashes with better melodies."

Drew stared toward the dance floor but didn't see Niki or Lee.

"The offer's still there if you're ready," Jasmine said. She held her keys.

"Oh," Drew blushed. "I just got out of something serious."

Her painted eyebrows bent. "Do I look like I'm trying to get married again?"

Drew finished his drink. "Sorry. I have zero idea what I'm doing."

Niki emerged from the crowd, like a fairy in a haunted forest. "C'mon," she said and pulled Drew to the dance floor.

"I'm saving you," she said in his ear. "She can be dangerous."

Niki's face was flawless and beautiful. She was no longer a child too young to legally drink. Flashing neon lights danced on her cheeks, and she wrapped her arms around him.

"Just dance with me a little."

Drew could barely hear her, so he leaned in. She raised her head and they locked eyes. Then she moved her forehead toward his until they touched.

Drew's heart pounded faster than the booming beats all around them. His arms were around her tiny waistline, her outfit's thin fabric light against his palms. It felt incredible to hold her and feel in control.

A new beat dropped and everyone screamed. Drew stumbled as some oaf in a white Celtics jersey bumped him from behind.

Snapping out of their trance, Niki smiled. He followed her back to the table, where her friends had also returned.

"Catch up," Lee said as he slid two small plastic cups over to Drew. They smelled too fruity to be straight liquor.

Drew emptied both to a cheer from his table, and he tried to stay positioned near Niki. A fearless euphoria from the alcohol built inside him, and he wondered if they could go back on the dance floor.

Niki cupped her hand around Drew's ear. "I really enjoyed that."

They nodded at one another. A silent agreement of something beginning. She had to understand that he wanted her. He would protect her on nights like these.

Jasmine walked by right then and did the math.

"Oh, I get it," she said.

Drew felt wonderful. The liquor raced through his head, and he hadn't been this drunk since college which led to a night of puking in Kelly's apartment. Forget Kelly he thought as he blatantly stared at the opening near Niki's heart. He could learn to love someone much smaller. Look at how sexy her neck is, he whispered to himself. She was laughing with her friends about something. Content, he continued to sip from a cocktail he didn't remember ordering while the others talked shop.

A drink later, Lee noticed first. "Uh oh, Drew's wobbling," he said.

"I'm fine." Drew looked at his feet and saw four of them.

"You're getting Bambi on ice legs and I don't want you puking in my truck."

The night became a blur of laughs and blackouts. They asked if he wanted to stop for food. "I'll buy," he answered.

They did not stop for food. Instead, they drove straight home and Lee hoisted Drew over his shoulder and laid him down fully clothed in bed where he slept until morning.

When he awoke, he felt surprisingly refreshed and hangover-free. He tried to rewind the previous night. His clothes smelled like dry ice and cigarette smoke. His hand stamp was smeared. Still, it felt like the night was a success.

"Wow," he groaned, kicking off his shoes. No headache, nausea, or regrets. As he brushed his teeth, he smiled at himself in the mirror. The hand stamp had smeared onto his cheek, so he scrubbed it off. He knew he danced with Niki. He was certain she held his hand on the ride home. He remembered sitting next to her, and she not only held his hand, he also recalled rubbing her arm before he passed out. Maybe he passed out leaning against her.

After showering and pulling on his weekend sweats, he walked by her closed door. He'd claim a spot on the couch and wait for her to join him. If Niki didn't have other birthday plans, he would buy her flowers and treat her to dinner. Heck, she could keep the ring. She'd earned it.

He sprawled on the lumpy couch and found a nature show. He could feign sleep and let her lean against him on the couch. He shifted several times until he found what looked like a natural position that hogged just enough of the space to suggest inevitable contact if she joined him.

A few minutes later, he subtly increased the volume as the intro music to another episode of *Wild Africa* blared through the apartment. Sure enough, Niki's door popped open. Her slippers scraped the carpet on her march down the steps. He closed his eyes and waited as she walked past into the kitchen.

He could hear her bagel prep routine. The smell of cinnamon made his stomach growl, but he stayed motionless. The coffee maker clicked on. Maybe she was the one with the hangover.

"Wake up, sunshine," she said, wiggling between his legs.

"Morning," Drew greeted her.

"Jasmine texted me about you."

Drew shook his head. "Flattered, but not interested."

"She sure is. Called you a tease. How you feeling?"

"Stellar. I slept through the night. You?"

She shrugged. On the TV, a pack of zebras ran across the screen toward a sunrise.

Drew sat up. "Here, let me rearrange." Maybe she'd curl up next to him. They could establish a physical relationship the way it was meant to be. He'd rejected Jasmine right in front of her, she had to appreciate that. How many times must Niki have witnessed Jasmine or other friends disappearing with strange barflies?

Niki giggled as the TV show switched its focus to a den of tiger cubs. He let out a laugh of his own. This would be their thing.

He and Kelly had so many "things" together. Rituals, games, traditions. Spending weekends at her father's house (which he wouldn't miss). He recalled his favorite game with Kelly called "Gotta Go." When one of them was on the phone, the other would disrobe and walk past.

The person on the phone would be forced to instantly end the call with a "Gotta go!" and be rewarded for prioritizing the relationship over the phone conversation. It was fairly one-sided, Drew found. Kelly often rolled her eyes when Drew attempted to pull her away from an important business call. "I can't blow a chance to make hundreds of dollars because you suddenly want to get laid," she often said. Kelly had a perfect record, though. Drew always hung up. Then again, most of his phone calls involved arranging pickleball matches.

Maybe someday he'd adapt that tradition with Niki, and it wouldn't be such a one-way street. Or better yet, they'd start their own traditions. He loved her cute giggling. Kelly never laughed at the television, even during sitcoms. "None of this is plausible," she'd say. Then her phone would ring and she'd miss the rest of the episode for a business call.

The coffee pot gurgled from the kitchen. "Want a cup?" Niki asked. "It's French vanilla."

"I'm good, thanks." Drew didn't want to hold a cup of coffee. He wanted to hold her and make the morning last forever.

"Coffee!" howled someone from upstairs. Drew jumped from the familiar voice that thundered from above.

Lee rumbled down the steps, causing each one to squeak and strain beneath his dirty boots.

"But first a moment with the Marlboro Man," he said, pounding a box of cigarettes. Lee's jeans sagged and his undershirt revealed hairy shoulders. He cracked his back, then his neck, then his knuckles. A soothing symphony it was not.

Niki disappeared into the kitchen as Drew felt himself sink into the couch. Maybe Lee slept on her floor to avoid the overnight DUI patrols.

Drew felt a resurgence of a hangover, like his heart was pumping toxins through his unprepared body.

Lee stepped back inside the door, followed by his cigarette cloud. Niki reappeared and carried a coffee cup with both hands over to him.

"Thanks, babe," Lee said.

Niki stood on her toes for a brief kiss on the lips.

"I'll text you," Lee said.

She nodded and rubbed her hands on his sides. Then they kissed again holding their lips together a little longer.

Finally, Lee left, his truck's loud engine disturbing the peaceful Saturday morning. Drew could do nothing but stare. Niki noticed. He could tell she wanted to say something but she didn't.

She disappeared up the steps and slammed shut her bedroom door.

Drew walked into the kitchen, removed the lid from the trash, leaned over, and puked so violently his eyes watered. Sweaty and exhausted, he collapsed on the couch. He felt like he was about to pass out when his phone buzzed. A text from Kelly.

"Are you seriously standing me up?"

He forced himself to conjure an appropriate response for ghosting the love of his life, but the best he could come up with was the truth.

"Sorry. Got sick this morning and have been puking in the kitchen garbage."

He pictured Kelly by herself in the gym waiting for him to appear and then informing the tournament official her partner was a no-show. Then every man there would console her or offer to fill in. They'd win the tournament, find common interests, and arrange to have dinner. She'd kiss him, but tell him she wanted to take it slow. Maybe they could play pickleball at her gym one morning if he didn't mind running into her ex-boyfriend who had ridden her coattails, but thankfully she was through with him.

She would never forgive him. Beautiful people don't have to forgive people the way they are always forgiven. Drew returned to his bedroom, puked in the wastebasket, and dwelled on these thoughts as his boomerang hangover worsened.

Why would she choose a guy like Lee? The worst part was Drew couldn't tell Charlie about this soap opera without a shit-ton of fallout.

All Drew's faraway buddy had asked was that he protect Niki for one night.

Drew had one job, and he was worse at it than his actual job.

12

An odd sense of post-hangover relief fell upon Drew as he passed Kelly's parked SUV on his way into the branch Monday morning. There was nothing else he could do to make this better. The hope was gone. If he was going to start life over without her, he would at least take care of the professional side of it. Other people got "lost in their work," maybe he could too.

"Great job last week," Craig said when the two met in his office. "Our numbers didn't miss a beat while I was out of the branch."

He set down a folded piece of paper on Drew's desk.

"Muchas gracias for remembering to put everything in my number."

Drew opened the sheet. It was a twenty-five-dollar gift card to The Cheesecake Factory. He feigned a smile and gave Craig an appreciative nod.

"You got a Superstar Comment from a customer too, buddy. Those look good when raise time rolls around." This was the friendliest his boss had ever been.

"And I believe it's warm enough that I won't need a jacket today. Keep up the good work," Craig said as he waved to the tellers and left.

Drew opened three checking accounts that morning before closing a loan on a new Escalade for a grouchy older lady who didn't smile until the cashier's check was in her tiny fists.

Like his coworkers already had, Drew resented his former lazy self. With each interaction, he began to realize his capabilities and potential. He found himself smiling and looking forward to helping every customer. He noticed the tellers exchanging glances and mumbling about "the new Drew," which embarrassed him.

Still, he knew someone very angry was upstairs, and that he would have to face her wrath. The morning felt like a ten-mile hike, and Drew was considering skipping lunch for a nap in his car when his desk phone rang. It was Kelly.

"Can you come up here?"

"In a bit. I have to finish a few things first."

"Are you feeling better?"

Concern was the last thing he expected.

"Much better. Sorry again about—"

"Good. Just come up when you can."

Dew put the phone down slowly then fumbled the receiver, unaware of how long he stared into space.

"Everything okay?" one of the tellers called.

"I think so."

Drew collected himself and told the teller line that if they needed him to call upstairs right away. They knew which office.

Kelly was typing when he knocked on her open door.

"Come in."

Cautious, he sat. "Sorry about Saturday."

Kelly rested her chin on her folded hands. "Who are you living with?"

"A friend of Lee's." Truthful. "Actually, Lee's girlfriend, Niki."

Her head tilted. Kelly made an O with her mouth and twisted her tongue. "Okay. That's what I heard."

"Then why are you asking?"

She'd already relayed the info to his mother, but Kelly didn't need to know how that went. Give away as little as possible, Drew thought. "Did Devlinger mention it?"

Her nose twitched like a tell in poker. "What's the arrangement?"

His voice became monotone. "Her brother got shipped overseas. It's an under-the-table sub-lease."

"So it's just you ... living with her."

"I don't think Craig even knows her, so whatever you're hearing—"

"He knows her."

Stomach pit. Certainly, Craig had never caught Niki's attention. If that was the case, his crush was over. Kaput. Eww.

"Well, she's dating Lee, so …"

"I didn't know Lee had a girlfriend. How long has that been going on?"

"As of this weekend."

"Classy," Kelly said. She picked up a pen.

"How does Craig even know her?"

She looked Drew directly in the eyes. "Playoffs. Like I said, classy."

"Craig's happily married to Mrs. Devlinger, so …"

Kelly huffed. "You men."

Drew shrugged. "It's not my job to defend the male species, which, unfortunately, includes Craig. Now, if you'll excuse me, this man has to get back to work."

Kelly's eyebrows raised. "Isn't Dev still down there?"

"Are we allowed to call him that?"

"I can call him whatever I want. He's not in charge of my department."

"He's visiting dealerships. I close the loans now and put them in his number."

"Why?"

"I'm training."

"No, why are you putting them in his number and not yours?"

"I don't have a number." Drew was about to leave when he turned back. "Do I?"

Kelly smirked. "You'd never be able to keep this job without me."

"As long as you aim me in the right direction when you belittle me, that's fine."

"And he's at a dealership today?"

"Probably for the rest of the afternoon."

"What time is the first pitch?"

"Sales pitch?"

"At Wrigley."

On his way downstairs, Drew couldn't decide whether to take Kelly seriously. He sure as hell wasn't going to accuse his boss of anything shady. One thing she was serious about was that he had a sales number. A quick call to human resources led to Drew discovering he was number 815.

Another surprise was that Kelly was talking to him. It was progress. Was it that he was learning a new role or was she jealous, not just envious, of his new roommate? He could survive a few more months of training, and then once an opening for a banker became available at another branch he would earn twice as much or more depending on bonuses, however the hell those were calculated.

That Friday, Craig wasn't around until late afternoon. He called Drew into his office.

"Shut the door, buddy." Craig leaned back and put his hands on his head. "Have a seat and self-evaluate how you're doing."

"I think I'm doing everything well enough." Earlier that week, there were one or two customers who had grown impatient with him as he worked his way through setting up their accounts, but Drew didn't see that as a reason for Craig to lose faith.

"Well enough for what?"

"To run the show while you're at the dealerships."

Craig nodded. "But are you feeling confident?"

"Yes. Did I mess anything up?"

Craig laughed as if Drew was a child who unknowingly said something adorable. "Think hard."

Drew's eyes shot to the ceiling, then back to Craig's nameplate. He thought about how Kelly called him "Dev" and wished he could be as informal.

"I think I've been doing better than expected."

Craig shifted in his chair then leaned forward. "Adams called about some customer feedback, Drew. Not the Superstar Bullshit, but a phone call straight from Adams."

Drew thought back again. Every customer seemed satisfied when they shook hands on the deals. He thought about when Kelly used to get mad at him. He'd retrace everything back to the last time they had sex and go from there to figure out what she was upset about. There was no method for this instance though.

Craig Devlinger held a cold expression as Drew's face reddened.

"What did I do wrong, Craig? Just tell me."

His boss laughed. "I didn't say you did anything wrong. In fact, it was about positive feedback. I don't know if it's all directed at you. I mean, the tellers get these compliments sometimes, but there must have been an excessive amount because Adams brought them all to my attention."

"I'm not in trouble?"

"God kid, I just explained it. You're almost doing too well."

Drew smiled. Kelly always told him he was a people person, but he never believed her.

Craig reverted back to a serious tone. "There's something else. What I'm about to tell you stays between us, okay?"

Drew nodded.

"I'm taking vacation next week."

Drew waited for more. "That's it? Won't people figure something's up when you're gone?"

"My wife and I have had some issues lately, and that's nobody's business. So if anyone asks, tell them I'm not at the branch right now. Or I'm backed up with loans, or whatever. Pretend I'm at a dealership and try to handle whatever it is yourself. You can do that for me, can't you?"

"Will the tellers know?"

"I'm not saying jack shit to those hens. You shouldn't either. They know it's not like me to take vacation, so they'll start their own rumors and then it gets upstairs, and before you know it the whole building is gossiping about my marriage."

Drew inadvertently glanced at the Devlinger family portrait. The happy parents held such genuine smiles.

Craig noticed his glance and picked up the photo. "Marriage always seems like a good idea, but … that's why you shouldn't be upset about not marrying Kelly. Once life happens, it's easy to lose that spark."

"Kelly and I are slowly mending things," Drew said evenly to hide his anger.

Another condescending laugh. "Not with that hot little roommate of yours, you're not."

"You know Niki?"

"She's been at my service a few times."

Drew Craig flirting with Niki and putting his arm around her. Craig kissing her. Craig pulling her shirt off. It couldn't be true. Yes, Lee was doing all of those things, but if she ever did anything like that with Craig, the attraction to her would disintegrate.

"She's with Lee now," Drew said, trying to turn his imagination off.

"For this week. You know how our boy is. She's too young and dumb to keep up with him."

Drew pretended not to care. "Don't worry about it and get out of here. Enjoy some quality time with your wife."

"I should focus on her instead of work for a week. But if anyone asks …"

Drew pantomimed zipping his lips.

***

Drew left work a little soured. He'd looked up to his boss, with his wife, two kids, home, and a good career. What more did a man need? He couldn't comprehend why his boss wasn't satisfied with what he had.

Drew struggled to shake the image of Craig touching Niki because it infuriated him. The warmer spring weather was here, and he sweated throughout his drive home. As he waited for the car's air conditioning to kick in, he tried to think about anything else. Could he beat Bull in singles? Which bourbon should he buy next? Would the Cubs win the pennant without divine intervention?

The apartment parking lot was crowded, so he settled for a vacant spot the next building over. When he turned off his engine, he saw Niki leaving.

She was in her Playoffs outfit. No jacket or warm-up pants, just boy shorts and a tank top not much larger than a sports bra. Drew was almost panting by the time she reached her car. He could've gotten out and said hi, but he suspected he'd make a fool of himself.

She drove off, the tail lights of her silver Versa fading quickly, oblivious to his desire. He let his heart slow down before he walked to the door. It was unlocked. Inside, Lee was sprawled on the couch. Drew didn't realize Niki was fine with Lee hanging out in the apartment when no one else was there, and Drew wondered if Lee kicked in for Niki's share of the rent.

Soured further, Drew walked into the kitchen without a greeting. Lee stayed quiet too. Did this guy ever feel awkward? Drew couldn't stand the dull tension.

"Hey, how close are you and Devlinger?" Drew finally asked.

Lee grinned. "Sounds like he told you about next week."

Drew walked to the edge of the living room. "Yes. Is his marriage okay?"

Lee shrugged. "None of my business. I just do what he says."

"I mean, if he's going to Playoffs all the time …" Drew tried to get a read on Lee, but he was more concerned with flipping stations. *Road House* was airing.

"Craig don't mess with none of them waitresses."

"You better hope not," Drew said, and they quietly spent the next half hour watching Patrick Swayze beat up the bad guys.

13

Day three without Craig was anything but a typical Wednesday. Drew stared at his computer screen for over ten minutes even though his shift had already ended.

"Are you almost done? Can I leave yet?" one of the tellers asked across the lobby. He looked up. It was the teller with glasses. Maybe Melanie? The rest had left, but it was against policy to leave someone alone in the bank lobby.

"Almost done," Drew barked. He had just closed the branch's largest loan in maybe a year.

A man named Jay Woods entered the branch around two p.m. asking for Drew by name. It took only a few moments for Drew to recall that one of Charlie's friends needed a loan for a boat. The principal amount was a behemoth one hundred twenty-three thousand, two hundred dollars. Even though Drew knew the subtle differences between car and boat loans, he called upstairs to underwriting to make sure the interest rate was correct.

Jay was friendly and patient, but Drew knew his shaking hands gave away how green he was at pulling this off.

While the lobby doors locked at five, Drew explained the loan details and had Jay sign all of the necessary forms. He turned the title over to Drew, who walked over to the unenthused teller to get the cashier's check for more money than Drew had ever hoped to hold in his hands.

"Congratulations on your boat, sir," Drew said, his handshake firm as ever.

Jay left, giddy about his new purchase, and Drew organized all the documents for headquarters. He triple-checked his work and felt it was flawless. By quarter till six, the remaining teller couldn't possibly keep her patience as Drew labored over whose number to enter the loan under.

On one hand, Craig specifically said to always use his number, 790. No exceptions.

Kelly revealed that Drew had his own number. Wasn't this loan completely his doing? His friendship with Charlie was why Jay chose Midwest. Jay could have gone to his own bank if he wanted, but Charlie told him he'd get a better rate through Drew. Craig didn't deserve any bonus while vacationing who knows where. Maybe Craig would never find out about the loan. Maybe he'd understand Drew deserved it.

Or perhaps Craig would become infuriated.

"Enter Sale ID," beckoned the prompt on the computer screen. He typed in 790 but couldn't get himself to hit enter.

It was almost six o'clock when Drew changed it to 815. What would the bonus be worth? Ten dollars? Fifty? Was it worth risking his job over?

Maybe he could play dumb. No, Craig would see through it.

Kelly would tell Drew to use his own number and tell Craig to get over it.

Click. Drew's 815 was entered into the system.

Drew could feel the teller's glare from across the lobby as he shut down his computer.

"Thank you so much for staying late. I really appreciate it, Melanie."

"I'm Jackie."

"Oh! My mistake. Now, I remember, I saw Melanie leave with everyone else."

"Melanie was out sick today."

As Jackie/Melanie stormed out the doors, Drew found himself nodding at Kelly's banner before turning off the lights.

Drew caught himself speed walking to his car. Though proud of working an extra hour, the regret of his decision weighed on him. He'd tell Craig it was a mistake. They could fix it online, right?

When a voice yelled, "Hey!" from across the lot, Drew jumped.

"Easy, tiger. Why are you here so late? Fall asleep behind your desk?" Kelly casually walked over in a dark gray pencil skirt. Drew glanced at her legs.

The adrenaline still pumping from his decision didn't relent. "I had to close a rather large loan."

Kelly playfully pushed a thumb into his chest and straightened his tie. "Look at you doing real work. Devlinger went home early?"

Drew never could hide things from her all that well. Christmas presents, vacation plans, and any other secrets found their way to Kelly no matter how hard he tried. "He must have."

"I haven't seen him all week."

Kelly squinted when Drew didn't respond. "What are you not telling me?"

"I put the loan in my number."

"You think he'll care?"

"It was for one hundred and twenty-three thousand dollars."

"Drew, are you serious?"

He nodded. When was the last time she was so impressed by something he'd done?

She hugged him. "I'm so proud of you."

She hugged him again, this time longer. Her cheek pressed into his and it turned him on. The faint smell of perfume and her hair held such familiarity. He realized how long it had been since experiencing any meaningful affection.

"I knew you had it in you." She smiled in a manner that reminded him of before they lived together when careers and bills and responsibilities never intruded.

"You think he'll be mad?" Drew asked.

"Yes." She let out a laugh, while Drew didn't find it as funny. "But if he gives you any shit tomorrow, let me—what?"

Drew opened his mouth but nothing came out.

Kelly's tone changed. "He's been gone all week, hasn't he?"

Drew thought back to the stern warning Craig gave. But Lee knew already. And Kelly didn't have time to gossip or worry about office politics.

"He's on vacation," Drew said.

"What? He doesn't take those."

"I know, but he's trying to …"

"Yes?"

"He went somewhere with his wife."

"Oh." Was she disappointed that that's all it was?

"He wanted to keep it a secret so that the tellers … You know how they are."

She nodded with her eyes closed. "I should get going."

She walked back to her SUV at the front of the lot then paused after opening the door. "Hey, I might have something to talk to you about soon."

"What?" There was a distance between them, so Drew almost yelled it. Then he remembered her dangling carrot routine.

"It's a job opportunity. Not personal. Actually, I guess it would be personal, since it's, you know, us."

"Whenever." Drew said. He wasn't going to beg for information. Kelly often withheld their plans until the last minute. It made him feel like a child, and he was done with that dynamic.

"I'll find you soon." She gave him one more big smile. "I know where you work."

As she drove off, Drew's remorse disappeared. Now he was as giddy as Jay. Maybe Kelly was returning to her old self. He could label it progress.

If Craig blew up on him about credit for the loan, at least Kelly would understand how he lost his job.

***

On his way home, Drew stopped at Jean's Deli, his favorite place for carryout wings. There was no reason to fear running into Kelly in public anymore. Niki was scheduled to work, so he decided to watch the Cubs game and chase dinner with a few bottles of Dos Equis. The warmer air outside allowed him to crack open a window in the living room. The days grew longer, and spring packed winter away for the year.

The wings were spicy, the Cubs were flat and clunky. Drew wished Niki was home, but it would still be hours. His beer buzz told him to text her about Charlie's friend getting the boat loan.

He was shocked when she replied immediately. "You should video chat with him tonight. He'd love that."

"Are you telling me I can play in your room?"

"You can use my tablet! Just don't steal any of my makeup!"

Tipsy and charmed by all the exclamation points, Drew washed the sauce from his hands and entered Niki's bedroom. As usual, a mysterious smell lingered from a candle—something with sandalwood and lemongrass. Everything about her was an exotic scent he couldn't get enough of. Drew picked up a bottle of her lotion and smelled the cap before feeling self-conscious. He wanted to learn everything about her. He wanted to be able to look at her whenever he wanted. He wanted to memorize her.

"I owe you big time," Drew told Charlie once they were connected.

"Jay already messaged me a picture of the boat." Charlie looked tired, sunburnt, and more wrinkled than the last time they talked. "You got time for another loan? I know plenty of my boys who will turn it into a pissing contest on not just who can buy the biggest boat, but who can get the best rate."

"Send them my way," Drew said. "I'll get in trouble, but it's worth it." He then explained that Craig would probably complain about Drew taking credit for Jay's large account.

"Promise me you won't back down," Charlie said. "Is my sis home?"

"Still at work," Drew said. "I'm riding a nice beer buzz, so I'm not ready to crash yet."

Charlie's screen froze for a moment but then returned to normal. "Is she doing okay?"

"I think so."

"Can you tell though? She always acts happy, but …"

Drew wondered if Charlie knew about Lee. "Did she say anything about my mom's visit?"

Charlie shrugged. "Honestly, I haven't talked to her in a while. That's why I wondered if everything was okay."

"My mom brought dinner over one night and got a little nosy when Niki explained about your parents and how they're not really in the picture."

"Oh."

"Then my mom asked her about her job."

Charlie's head bobbed. "I hate that she works there, but dammit if she doesn't make a shitload of money. I can't protect her from the creeps, but she knows better. She's not like the other girls there."

Drew felt guilty for holding back about Lee, but he didn't want to spill the truth. Maybe Lee and Niki would break up before Charlie returned home. Instead, Charlie talked about his failed relationship. He explained in more detail this time that the six-month tours overseas were more than his marriage could handle.

"When the truth came out about the other man … God, it hurt worse than anything I've ever felt." He shrugged with a false grin. "You don't expect to be living with your little sister on your thirtieth birthday, but then there I was. I hope she's in a better situation by the end of her twenties. If she ends up with some loser, I'll blame myself."

Charlie's posture straightened. "Is she still seeing the one dude?"

Drew had no idea who the "one dude" was. Perhaps the guy she had friend-zoned. Either way he was jealous, but also glad Charlie was a hemisphere away. Otherwise he would have sensed something wrong with Drew's answer. "She's not. As far as I know. She didn't have a date on her birthday. Just me and Lee, and a couple guys who date the girls she works with."

"Honestly, and this is gonna sound weird," Charlie said as he leaned toward the camera, "I hope she can find a guy like you."

Drew pointed at himself with mock surprise and shrugged.

"I mean, not *YOU* you. That would be weird, and I know you're trying to get back with your ex." Charlie shook his head. "I don't want her ending up with a guy like our pops. My folks had me before they were married, and mom was so young that she never got to live out her fun years."

"So she took off?"

"She's out there living a life where she probably stays up later than Niki." Charlie laughed to himself and seemed to be reflecting on something. "I hope my sis breaks that cycle of getting tied down too soon. And if she does settle, I hope he's a good guy."

Drew wondered if his heart beat was visible through his shirt. Had Niki mentioned the possibility of her having feelings toward him to Charlie?

Charlie changed to an upbeat tone. "I bet your folks are better than mine. What's your pops like?"

"Irish Catholic."

"You get along?"

"He's not happy about my breakup with Kelly. Hasn't talked to me since."

"He'll see the light. Sounds like Kelly has everyone fooled."

Drew frowned. He didn't like the possibility of that phrase.

"Sorry, bud. But hey, if he ever meets Niki, she eats fathers for breakfast."

Drew tried to picture that encounter. For every question Maryann asked about Niki's job, Rick would drill about her faith. *"Have you ever stepped foot in a church? Are you baptized?"*

"Drew, you okay? Enough of this serious shit. How are the Cubs looking?"

Drew stammered an answer as the conversation shifted to baseball, but his mind never left the last topic. Charlie approved of him more than Kelly's father, more than his own father, and they hadn't even met in person.

For the next hour they discussed their childhoods and the games they'd attended. Charlie and Niki, natives of Pittsburgh, had an uncle who took them to hockey and baseball games. Drew brought up baseball cards and they discovered more similar hobbies. Charlie also liked Star Wars, Transformers, and even had a similar taste in music: grunge and anything with a good beat. By the time they wrapped up the conversation, Drew had a new close friend. Still, he withheld the secret about Lee, as well as his feelings toward Niki.

That night as he lay in bed, Drew felt a little gaga. Certainly, Charlie would ask Niki the same questions and plant the idea in her head. They must be close enough to discuss those types of things, so perhaps she'd reveal the truth about her relationship with Lee. He'd be disgusted, and set her straight with a brotherly scolding. Drew felt his eyes shutting just as his phone buzzed on the windowsill by his bed. He debated ignoring it completely, but rationalized that it might have been a health issue with one of his parents.

"You up?"

It was Kelly.

14

The first thing that surprised Drew was Kelly wanting to talk. The second surprise was that she wanted to talk in person, immediately. The kicker? She would drive to his place. He scrambled downstairs to straighten the couch cushions and wipe down the kitchen, but then decided he wanted her to feel uncomfortable.

When she arrived, he could tell she'd had two glasses of wine. Drew could easily guess with almost one hundred percent accuracy how many glasses she'd indulged, up to five. At two, she was slightly louder, more outgoing, and somewhat frisky.

"Is parking always this bad here?"

Drew ignored the question and led her into the kitchen. "All I have is beer."

"Eww," she said. "No."

He saw her peering at Niki's work schedule. "I'll show you the rest of the place," Drew said, but Kelly lingered as if memorizing the calendar. As they walked up the stairs, Drew worried Niki would come home. Kelly and Niki interacting would be too unpredictable. And when would Lee arrive? Word would get back to the branch, and the rumors would swirl. He'd closed Niki's door earlier, so Drew didn't acknowledge it as they walked down the hall.

"Here's my lair," he said. Kelly brushed by him and sat on his bed while he remained standing. She crossed her legs and leaned back on her hands.

"I've come into a business opportunity that might interest you." She spoke in a silly British accent, probably aware of how cliché she sounded.

Drew heard the door open downstairs, but Kelly didn't acknowledge it. At her higher volume, another barometer for glasses of wine, Kelly would be easy to hear from downstairs. "My dad and his partners are buying a small mortgage company."

"And you're going to run it," Drew said without emotion. His bedroom felt tiny. There was nowhere for him to sit.

"And I was thinking, since you're learning the ins and outs of banking so quickly, maybe you could do the same with mortgages."

Just then, Drew heard the familiar rumble of Lee's truck. He always seemed to land a closer parking spot. He pictured the buffoon lumbering in, never knocking anymore. Whenever Lee shut the door, the whole apartment shook.

Drew ignored it, hoping Kelly would too. Instead, she winced as the walls vibrated.

"When would you be leaving Midwest?"

Kelly shrugged. "Nothing is certain yet. But yes, there's ... stuff I need to get away from. I don't want to sound whiny."

The excuse sounded weak. Kelly's silver spoon was feeding her yet again.

"You'd make a lot more, if you can handle the workload."

"You have such a gift for being enticing and hurtful simultaneously."

Downstairs he heard Lee's voice and the microwave beeping. Kelly looked toward the door.

"What does this mean as far as us?" Drew asked.

Kelly looked around the room, as if she wanted to compare it to the one they used to share. Drew saw her head jerk back toward him like she was turning away from something obscene. The box on his dresser. It was closed, but still a reminder of what started this all. She sighed.

"I don't want to push you into anything. You left me, and that was your decision."

"Lots to consider," Drew said.

Kelly stood up and walked toward the dresser. Her back was to Drew but he knew she was opening the box and taking another look at what she declined.

"Definitely sleep on it. Take all the time you need."

Drew stood near her, and Kelly immediately hugged him.

"Why did you come here to bring all this up tonight?"

She pulled back. "I feel like I'm just figuring some things out. What I want in life, and what I don't need."

Drew noticed it was suspiciously quiet downstairs.

"I'll show myself out," Kelly said.

Drew tried to decide whether to follow her out. He figured it would be better to explain everything to Lee and Niki after Kelly departed. Maybe she would slip out the door without acknowledging them. Drew stood in his doorway holding his breath as she reached the stairs.

"Hey, Kelly-Bell!" Lee's voice echoed from downstairs. "Leaving already?"

"Howdy, Lee. Drew said I might be able to find some wine down here."

Drew walked toward the stairs and listened to what was going on.

"I'm Niki. Nice to meet you!"

"You have wine, right? These boys and their beer."

"Sorry, I'm beering it up too," Niki said.

"Of course you are, precious." He knew Kelly was making her twisted, snobby face.

Why wasn't she leaving?

"There's a few bottles of bourbon above the stove," Lee said.

"There is?" Niki asked.

"Yeah, Yellowstone Select. Good shit!"

Drew fumed. Of course Lee had invaded his collection. That particular bottle was never meant to be shared. Yet Drew's feet remained cemented in the upstairs hallway.

"You're out of ice," Kelly announced. "I'll bet I know who didn't refill the tray."

Moments later, Kelly was striding back up the steps.

"What are you doing?" Drew asked.

"Oh, like you don't want this too." She kicked the door shut and her shoe off in one swift motion.

She slammed the bourbon and tossed the glass to the floor. Then she shoved Drew onto the bed and started pulling his clothes off. First his T-shirt, then his sweat pants and drawers before looking around. "Sorry, I need to turn the lights off or this decor is going to cockblock you worse than a chubby friend at a nightclub."

She clicked off the switch, and with the little bit of light from the window Drew saw her pull her shirt off. Confused but aroused, he watched as she awkwardly spun her bra enough to unhook it. It was like she was disrobing to take a shower instead of foreplay.

"I'm still on the pill," she said, climbing on top of him.

Reluctant to stop her, Drew still tried to slow her. "You were on your way out two minutes ago."

"You missed me, didn't you?" She lowered her voice to a whisper and put her lips against his ears. "You missed this."

He peeked at her body and its familiar curves. One of her blonde hairs got caught in his mouth as she began grinding her hips on him. Despite the hiatus, he was going to last longer than usual. Kelly added to the delay by crying out as if faking it. Certainly they'd hear downstairs.

Ah-ha! thought Drew. One look at Niki and she felt threatened. Kelly's moans were beyond anything he'd heard from her. He even rolled his eyes while she continued. He had never been so self-conscious during sex. They might as well have been filming it. He knew she wouldn't stop until he finished. He tried picturing Kelly's bedroom and the numerous times they'd done it there. They had great chemistry most of the time, so it never took this long. Drew closed his eyes, trying to block everything out until it was over. Minutes later Kelly rolled off of him, breathing hard and laughing.

"Took you awhile, champ." She slapped his arm. "A little rusty?"

Drew nodded and got up from the bed before walking into the bathroom and turning on the shower. Pillow talk didn't sound appealing.

He couldn't look Kelly in the face. He could barely look at himself in the mirror. Finally, he inspected his own image. His collar was bright red from where Kelly had squeezed him like an animal. But it wasn't Kelly he was thinking of when he finally got off.

As soon as his mind imagined Niki, he lost control.

Kelly stayed and took up most of the full-sized mattress while Drew barely slept. With his eyes accustomed to the darkness, he gazed at her exposed left leg where the sheet didn't cover. He felt conquered. He had missed sex, of course, but then that wasn't exactly their best session. What did this mean for their relationship? The mortgage job sounded interesting, but he was just getting comfortable at the bank.

After tossing (there wasn't much room for turning) a while longer, he put on shorts and slipped downstairs. It was just after four, and he knew he wouldn't get much sleep next to Kelly.

He almost nodded off but heard a door open upstairs.

"Hey," a voice whispered from atop the steps. Niki tiptoed down and joined him on the couch. She wore an oversized Notre Dame T-shirt that stretched almost to her knees.

"She's interesting. What is going on up there?"

"No idea," Drew whispered back. "First she asked me about working with her, or rather for her at this new company, then she acted like she was going to leave."

"She had her keys in her hand but then asked for a drink."

"Weird." Drew recalled the naked image of Niki he used to get off.

"Is she always that … loud?" Niki squeaked out a laugh.

Drew turned away, shaking his head no.

"I don't know your woman, but she seems psycho."

"It's like she was trying to prove a point to me," Drew said. "Or herself."

"Or me," Niki said with a tiny snort.

Drew's eyes widened. Niki was wearing the ring.

"Oops, yeah. I wore it yesterday."

"Maybe she wants it back," Drew said.

"Right?" Niki said. She took it off for a moment and admired the diamond. Then she casually slipped it back on. "You aren't gonna move out and leave me?"

"If I do, it seems Lee will fill my spot. He's here most nights anyway. Apparently, sampling my bourbon collection free of charge."

"I'd throw him in the room you're using, as loud as he snores."

The complaint brought Drew a touch of joy.

She stood and walked toward the kitchen, where the light above the sink outlined her silhouette. She extended her arms above her to stretch, and her shirt raised to her upper thighs. Drew caught the bottom of her cheeks before she lowered her arms and took her glass off the table.

"I'll tell you what," she said, walking back into the living room and standing in front of him. He glanced at the legs he'd envisioned wrapped around him earlier. "If anything ever happens between you and me ..."

Niki looked back up the steps.

"We're dumping both of these losers."

Drew exhaled out the word, "Deal."

Footsteps came from upstairs. "Since when do you get up so early?" Kelly, dressed again in her clothes from when she arrived, made her way down the steps. She stopped on the last one when she saw Niki. "Forget your pants?"

"I live here," Niki said.

"Well," Kelly said, slapping her pant legs. "Think about what I said, Drew, and we'll get the ball rolling." She leaned over and kissed him on the mouth, morning breath and all. That was something she never did before they broke up. Why did she feel like a stranger? It may have been that for the first time in her life, Kelly Treader felt insecure.

She turned to Niki. "Good luck with Lee. What a keeper."

Niki held an unimpressed expression while Kelly slipped out the door. The sound of Kelly's car faded.

Niki got up and walked to the bottom of the stairs. "I meant what I said."

Drew watched her ascend before returning to his room. He slept until his alarm went off early enough for morning pickleball.

15

Drew glowered across the net at Bull.

For the first time ever he had game point, 10-9. Drew premeditated a strong serve to force a weak return and then hit a third-shot winner down the line to claim victory over his break-of-dawn nemesis. The two had fallen into an unspoken agreement to play every other day, and Drew sensed his first victory wasn't far off.

After a deep breath, he aimed and fired a serve to Bull's backhand. The return was powerless, but right as Drew approached the game-winning shot, an errant ball from an adjacent court rolled onto theirs.

"Ball!" Bull called. "Redo."

Drew collected himself and returned to his serving spot to replay the point.

Kelly walked in wearing purple yoga pants and a white tank top. It had been several days since her late-night visit, and they hadn't crossed paths at work or communicated over the weekend. The dudes who'd ruined Drew's last point paused their game to stare at her.

"Are you winning?" Kelly shouted.

Drew nodded. When he turned to serve, he could see his opponent smiling. Drew attempted the same deep serve to Bull's backhand. The ball bounced on the line.

"Out!" Bull called.

"What?"

"Just out." Bull held his fingers an inch apart. "Your wife know this one! One inch!" Bull howled.

Drew and Kelly exchanged a cringe.

Bull served and Drew fired his return to the back corner. Bull barely got to it, but made solid contact. The ball clipped the top of the net and fell straight down on Drew's side.

"Ten all, baby!" Bull chirped with a fist pump.

Drew shanked his return on Bull's next spin serve and now faced game point.

"You can do this," Kelly said. She sounded somewhat normal again. All weekend, Drew wondered if she'd been replaced by a clone.

"11-10," Bull announced, and then served. Drew's return was firm, but Bull chased it down. Drew stepped forward ready to volley Bull's shot, but again it hit the net. This time it only clipped the top and instead of trickling over, it shot over Drew's paddle and landed just in bounds.

He'd lost again.

"Haven't seen you in a long, long time," Bull said, turning toward Kelly instead of telling Drew good game.

She gave a faint smile then walked over to Drew and put an arm around him. "You got pretty lucky," she yelled back to Bull.

"Not as lucky as he did," Bull said. He pushed his palms together and bowed at Kelly.

Drew was visibly frustrated. "Guess it's time to hit the showers and head to work."

Kelly pulled back her arm and faced him. "I'm taking the morning off. My appointment canceled, so I'm running home to shower."

"Is that an invitation?" Drew wanted to ask. Part of him wanted to find out. Certainly back at their home base the sex would go much smoother. Maybe she wanted him to ask just so she could say no and reestablish control.

Instead, he huffed, "If you hadn't been watching, I could've closed him out."

"You'll get him next time. Second chances, right?" she said as she walked away.

It was hard not to blame Kelly for the loss. Still, there was a good chance they would play doubles again sometime. That was the goal, right?

16

Later that Monday morning, Drew parked next to Craig's Volvo and immediately felt a sense of panic, like passing a cop car in a school zone.

At his desk, Drew kept his head down, not allowing himself to look into Craig's office. When he did, he noticed how much paperwork swamped the desk. Craig stood while trying to get organized. Other than a sunburnt face, Drew couldn't tell his boss had spent the last week relaxing at the beach. A few minutes later, Drew tentatively entered Craig's office.

"Yes?" Craig said without looking up from the contents of a manila folder.

"Have a good trip?"

Craig finished reading a page. "Relaxing, to say the least."

"That's good. Listen, I—"

"So you can imagine my disappointment when I discovered you closed the largest loan of the quarter under your number instead of mine. Care to sit your ass down and explain?"

Drew remained standing. "It was a boat loan from an acquaintance. You were off the clock."

Craig stacked the papers together and tapped them against the desk. "Did I say you could do that? 'Hey Drew, while I'm gone, please steal money out of my bonus. Even though I've been nothing but patient and given you free training after being a bum for well over a year, please put the biggest loan you'll ever see under your name, not mine.' Did I say that?"

Drew hung his head. "No, sir."

"Sir? Oh, now you're going to show respect? If you pull this kind of shit again, I'll kick you out faster than Kelly did."

"Kelly didn't kick me out. You guys egged me on to leave."

"Get over her. She's over you." Craig waved his hand, brushing Drew out of the office.

"Not really," Drew said.

"Ha!" Craig fell into his chair, kicked a foot up and rested it on his other knee. "Do tell. Entertain me. Hell, let's call Kelly down and get the details."

"She's off this morning. Her appointment canceled."

This seemed to be all the proof Craig cared to hear. He stood up, establishing his slim height advantage. "I'm heading to the dealerships. There are two loans coming in.

My number. Seven. Nine. Zero. Don't you forget it or I'll have it tattooed on your unemployed ass."

Drew retreated to his desk. Maybe the Devlingers weren't able to mend their differences on vacation. Lee might know, but he didn't trust him enough to ask. Maybe a teller would catch wind of it and spill to Kelly once the trip was no longer a secret. Whatever happened, it turned Craig into an even bigger asshole.

Drew reflected how Craig was such an ally during his breakup, but now Kelly was the only one who would help him deal with Craig. If his boss took it too far, he could quit, work with Kelly, and live happily ever after with her.

"Craig, you might just be doing me a favor after all," Drew said as he logged on to his computer.

***

Drew increased the morning trips to the gym as the sun rose earlier, but he never encountered Kelly. He also couldn't break his losing streak against Bull.

At work, Craig grew more and more distant. Sometimes he was absent the entire day. However, the Devlinger car loan plan continued to work like a charm. Drew couldn't believe how high the interest rates were, but then again, the credit scores were scary too. He stopped worrying about getting fired and began enjoying his role again. Some customers believed he was in charge of the branch now.

Drew bantered with the tellers and the regulars who visited the branch multiple times a week. At the end of each day, when the tellers locked the lobby doors, Drew relaxed and felt gratified. He wasn't working as many hours as Kelly, but word of his new work ethic definitely reached her through the tellers. He smiled about that on his drive home.

One evening, Drew arrived at the apartment to find Lee on his couch digging through a box of Frosted Flakes with his hand.

"Niki got called into work," Lee said as Drew noticed a stench.

"Were you smoking in here?"

"What? No, it probably just drifted in."

The air conditioning hummed in the background. Had this dumbass turned on the AC and held the door open while he smoked?

"I was talking to Charlie," Drew said.

Lee flipped through the channels. "What's he up to?"

"Whatever he does over there," Drew said. "Does he know about …"

Lee turned the channel again. "What's that?"

"Does he know about you and Niki?"

"Beats me. You're the one who talks to him."

"What do you think he'll say if he found out when he comes home?"

"Who knows? That's months from now, right? We're not serious." Crumbs had gathered on Lee's stomach. "What's it to you, anyway?"

The question held a sharpness to it.

"Charlie asked me if Niki was still seeing the same guy, and I didn't know what to tell him. So I didn't mention it."

Lee nodded. "You minded your own business." He gave Drew a hard glare then stuffed his mouth with more cereal.

"You don't worry about what he'll think?"

Lee removed his hand from the box. "Partner, when I'm with someone, I don't worry about down the road or if she's the one. I play it by ear."

Absurd, Drew thought. He had Niki's heart and he wouldn't consider where the relationship was going. He would've rather asked the question about Charlie to Niki, but with Lee being over so often, it was rare to spend any alone time with her.

Drew sat at the other end of the couch as Lee continued to flip channels.

"Were you going to chip in on my bourbon collection you found in the cupboard?" Drew asked.

Lee strode into the kitchen, reached into a cupboard and pulled down an unopened bottle of Yellowstone Select.

"I got you, buddy. Texans don't take another man's property."

"Thank you. And sorry for the accusation." He tried to hide that he was ashamed, but he could feel that his face was red. "This is why I hate confrontation."

"I'm guessing because you never won an argument with Kelly," Lee laughed. "Feel like watching the Cubs versus White Sox?"

Drew prepped two bourbons on the rocks. Five innings later, Niki arrived home.

"What a fucking night," she said.

Drew's jaw dropped at her appearance. She wore skin-tight boy shorts and a long-sleeved top that was just as snug. Everything was black except the sides, which were a shiny silver. Her abs were toned and as bronze as the rest of her skin. Drew wanted to stare forever, but his eyes consciously returned to the screen. Niki must have sensed his quick gaze, because she made a point to stand just off to the side of the television.

"You guys start a party without me? No fair."

She plopped down on Lee's lap and put her arm around him. Drew felt his heart bruise. Her legs extended toward him and she kicked off her sneakers.

"You make good dough off the chumps today?" Lee asked her.

Her head dropped onto his shoulder. "Not half as much as I deserve." He kissed her on the cheek as a Cubs rookie who was touted as the second coming of Christ grounded into a double-play.

Drew quickly sipped his bourbon. It didn't taste as smooth as usual, but enough of it could numb his bottomless pit of jealousy. He considered retreating upstairs, but wanted to hear if Lee would bring up his question about Charlie to Niki.

Instead, Niki ranted about her tables while the Cubs fell further behind their Southside rivals. During a pitching change in the seventh, Lee told Niki he needed to get up for a smoke.

"Wait," she pleaded. "I don't feel like moving."

"C'mon," he said, taking his pack out.

She remained curled in his lap. Drew relished their tiff and decided if she ever clung onto him like that he'd never move.

"You know I need a smoke when I drink," he said.

"Maybe I'll sit on Drew's lap," she said.

Drew did his best not to react, but his heart rate tripled. He took another swig and realized he'd already finished the drink. Half an ice cube circled the bottom of his Army cup. He'd ask Kelly whatever happened to his Northwestern cup next time they spoke as an excuse to reminisce about that day.

"Tell you what," Lee said. "If that's what it takes to get to my next smoke." He cradled Niki in his arms, set her on Drew's lap and let out a laugh.

"Are you insane?" Drew said, acting as though he was playing along.

Niki giggled and settled onto Drew, then stuck her tongue out at her man. She put her arm around Drew, pressing her head against his. He could smell her breath as it triggered some primal attraction. She was so feathery light and her neck smelled of the exotic spice from the scents in her room.

"Oh God, he's so warm," she purred. "He's like a furnace."

"Probably from the liquor," Drew said.

"Don't smother him," Lee said as he headed out the door. As always, he slammed it and rattled the walls.

An obnoxious commercial from a used car dealership Drew recognized came on the air. The salesman swung a guitar and promised the deal of the century. Niki sighed, and Drew felt her squeeze the muscle on the front of his shoulder.

Was she really committing to this? For all Drew cared, Lee could smoke an entire carton, catch emphysema and die out there.

Drew steadied his breathing, but he knew his heart beat through his chest like he'd just sprinted a mile.

"Oh," Niki whispered. "Your heartbeat is …"

"I know," he said, turning his head away.

Her hand slid from his shoulder to his chest like she was taking his pulse.

"I didn't know," she said, and calmly climbed back to the other side of the couch. She pulled a leg up, rested her forehead on her knee, and gave Drew a tiny smile.

They sat in silence until Lee returned.

"Anybody score?" He was the only one who laughed. "Better not have!" He laughed louder.

His cigarette still glowed in his hand. He dropped it next to the doormat and snuffed it out with his foot.

The game was all but over. His contact with Niki was over. He didn't need to drink anymore.

"I think I'll call it a night," Drew said. "The Cubs aren't pulling this one out."

"What? Stopping at two?" Lee said.

"We've had way more than that. Besides, I have a big match tomorrow morning."

"Oh, well. Nighty night," Lee said in a mocking voice.

Niki stayed quiet. She gave the same little smile as earlier without looking at him.

Drew walked up the steps, his pulse still racing.

17

The bank was closed on Memorial Day, but Niki still had to work a dinner shift. She scrambled around upstairs pulling her uniform out of the dryer.

"I hope none of that shrunk in the wash," Drew said, but Niki didn't laugh.

Drew was content to lounge in the living room watching the Cubs game. The team's pitchers were observing the holiday by ignoring the strike zone except for a hanging slider that a Met leadoff hitter bashed to the far side of Sheffield Avenue.

He overheard Niki's conversation upstairs and figured she was on a chat with Charlie. When she came down, she wore sweatpants but nothing over her work top. The white top complimented her tan complexion.

"I need to head out soon," she said, slightly out of breath and applying lip gloss. "But Charlie is still online if you want to talk."

He hurried up the steps into Niki's open room.

"Drew, my man! My buddy is raving about that rate you got him."

"And my boss still wants to kill me."

"What's your plan if he fires you? Another bank?"

"Sort of. Kelly mentioned something about working at a mortgage company her dad might buy."

"Is that what you want to do?"

Drew looked at his shoes for an answer.

"Doesn't sound like it is. What happened? Sounds like you two are talking again at least. Before you would've gone back to her in a second."

"I don't know," Drew said as he noticed a lavender pair of Niki's panties on the floor. "I really like where I'm at. The bank, I mean."

"Can you say no to her job offer, but yes to her?"

"Maybe. She seemed impressed when I closed your buddy's loan." Drew tried to remain poker-faced for his next question. "Did Niki tell you Kelly spent the night here?"

Charlie burst out laughing. "No! You broke up, barely talked, and then suddenly you're bouncing bedsprings again?"

Charlie rested his chin on his fists. He squinted and scratched his head. His expression turned pained. "My ex-wife tried the same thing."

Drew froze.

"Here's what's going on. Kelly was seeing someone else and it didn't work out. Now, you're her backup plan, buddy."

Drew now felt ill. A second glance at the lavender panties did not cheer him up.

"I'd be super careful. I mean, if you can get over the fact your dream gal was, you know … unfaithful."

"It kills me to think about it. Who would be good enough for her standards? And when would they hook up? She's not at the gym much anymore, but it doesn't mean she's having a sunrise-only affair."

"Sure. Maybe she bought one of those expensive exercise bikes."

"Either way, I don't plan on moving back in with her until we're engaged."

"Our lease expires in the fall where you're at. If we need to, you and I could find a bigger place when I get back."

"Really?" Drew was touched by the offer.

"Rent something closer to Wrigley Field, maybe."

"What about Niki?"

"Up to her. I think she's got more money than me. She'll be fine anywhere on—Oh my God, you're in love with my sister."

Drew didn't flinch. Maybe Charlie was kidding.

"Did something happen?" Charlie rubbed his shaved head.

"I swear, nothing's ever happened."

Charlie leaned back and looked to his left for some reason before turning his attention back to Drew.

"She's acting … coy. Maybe it's nothing." Charlie looked like he was trying to solve a math problem without any paper. "If anything ever happened to me, I'd want her to be with a guy like you. But with her …"

Drew waited intently for any insight.

"With her you gotta … hmm. How can I put this? My sister gets scared by guys easily because they fall for her pretty quickly."

"No shit."

"Been that way since high school."

She didn't seem scared of Lee, Drew thought. What had he done that was so special? Nothing. And that's what worked.

"If I'm correct about you having feelings for her, you better tone 'em back is what I mean. She's only twenty."

"Twenty-one."

"Oh yeah, twenty-one. She's not looking to get into anything serious. I've heard her complain about guys pulling that shit over and over."

What Charlie didn't know is that she had trapped herself in a casual relationship with a smoky slob who didn't deserve her. I should just tell him the truth, Drew thought. But he didn't. He suddenly felt self-conscious in Niki's room.

"One more thing," Charlie said. "Back to the boat loans. Jay's cousin wants one too, but bigger. You know how these pissing contests get."

"Yes, I do."

***

Even with minimal interaction, Drew still felt like he was in the Devlinger Doghouse. When Lee stopped at his desk, Drew welcomed the company. "Boss out today?"

"Back at the dealerships. I'm closing two more loans, so I guess it's working."

Lee didn't seem impressed. "I talked to Charlie."

It took Drew a moment to register Lee's stern tone.

"He said you and him clicked pretty well, but you seemed lonely without Kelly."

"Yeah?" There was no way Charlie said that.

"I told him about Niki's friend Jasmine. You remember her?"

Drew chuckled. "Jasmine O'Keeffe, you mean. Friendly girl. Fine Irish spirit."

"Here's the thing." Lee was now smiling. "I kind of promised her something."

"What?"

"Your number."

"That's fine. Just don't tell Kelly."

"Also," Lee said as he cracked his neck, "we made a bet as to whether you'd go out with her."

"Go out. With her?"

"And I wanted the apartment for us on Friday, so …"

"You told her I'd go out with her?"

"Bet, not told."

"What was the wager?"

"She has to cover my next tab at Playoffs."

"What do I get out of it?"

"Play your cards right and—"

"How did this even come up?"

Lee rubbed his face. "She was busting my balls about Niki living with another guy. She thinks ... you know."

This was an orchestrated lie. Would it be easier just to go along with the scheme? Kelly wouldn't find out. Or maybe she should. If she was jealous of Niki, she'd be jealous of anyone.

Drew thought back to Niki's birthday. Niki practically pulled him away from Jasmine and danced with him. Her jealousy was inevitable, too.

Drew hesitated. "Jasmine is too forward. Too old. Too ... divorced."

"You're not one of those guys who only dates white girls, are you? Because man, you're definitely missing out if you're racist."

Drew blushed. "Racist?" The tellers looked over.

"You know what? Yes, I'll go out with her if she texts."

Lee's eyebrows shot up. "There's my man! Let her slide into your DMs and you can slide into her ..." He rubbed his hands together slowly.

"Good God, Lee. Just tell her to text me."

By the time Drew left work, he and Jasmine arranged to meet at her place Friday night.

It felt good to be wanted.

18

Drew pulled into an impressive home at the address Jasmine O'Keeffe sent him.

"How much did these servers make?" Drew asked himself as he cut the engine.

It was a large, modern-looking brick home in a safe neighborhood where everyone's ground lights illuminated their yard's landscaping.

The doorbell chimed three chords. Perhaps he'd completely misjudged Jasmine O'Keeffe. Was she a stripper too? They pulled in thousands of dollars a week. Maybe she was a successful day-trader who only worked at Playoffs to boost her self-esteem.

Jasmine O'Keeffe answered the door in a loose-fitting, light gray sweat suit. It slipped off and exposed her left shoulder. She greeted him with a peck on the cheek. As he followed her through a family room, he noticed her tugging at her sweats to stay up.

"Beautiful home."

She laughed. "Let me make sure the kids are in bed."

Drew gulped.

"Don't worry, they're not mine. Make yourself comfortable on the couch."

Drew scanned the living room. No pictures, just paintings of mountains and prairies. It looked like a display model home. He sat on the couch, careful not to kick the half-full wine glass on the floor. What was Niki pulling in from these carefree businessmen?

She hurried back downstairs. "You're probably wondering whose house you're in."

"Yours?"

"My ex-husband's."

A sweat broke out under Drew's arms, and he glanced back to the door.

"I'm kidding, silly. Mr. O'Keeffe couldn't afford a house like this. Belongs to a girlfriend I live with. Not a *girlfriend*, girlfriend, so no three-ways for you dear. A friend since high school. I guess you could say it was her ex-husband's house."

Jasmine O'Keeffe adjusted her sweats again and joined Drew on the couch.

Why did she have to mislead him so much? The game wasn't fun.

"So you've got roommates too."

"Two little ones and Kim, but she won't be back until the early morning."

She leaned in playfully on Drew. Her hair felt stiff, like it had been oversprayed. "Want a beer?"

"No. Wait, yes."

She laughed. "Are you unsure or nervous?"

"Both?"

Drew watched her slink back into a kitchen that could only be rivaled by the one at Terry Treader's house.

"I'm more of a wine drinker," Jasmine said. Just like Kelly, he thought.

She returned to the couch with a can of an IPA he'd never heard of and a bottle of cabernet. Drew regretted not asking for bourbon. He wondered if he could've scored a solid pour here.

Jasmine settled in and tucked her legs to the side making just a touch of contact. It softened him somewhat.

"If you're okay with just kicking it here, we can see what's on," she said, flipping the channels. "Does *Jeopardy* work?"

"I catch it sometimes." He and Kelly used to watch it almost daily on the DVR. If it was a busy week, they'd catch up at her parent's house where Kelly and Terry would destroy Drew every time. Unless music or sports came up, he wasn't quick enough to answer before them.

That was not the case with Jasmine. Heading into the first commercial break, he was answering about two out of every three as she sat stunned. "Oh my God, smarty-pants."

"Give yourself some credit that you knew the one about the *Fast and the Furious* movies."

"How do you know all this stuff?"

"College was good for something." The beer fueled his confidence.

"Shut up! Where did you go?"

"Northwestern." Was she really that impressed? Then he thought about those two dude-bros at Niki's birthday, and how she probably dated that type.

"Intelligence is like my number one turn-on in a man."

When she leaned on him, he could smell the wine.

Drew tried to relax, but yet again his trusty ticker pounded away. He had to admit, she was charming. But he was afraid of where the night would go, and she was getting tipsy. When she poured her next glass, she looked at him instead of the bottle.

Drew turned his attention to the TV and resumed his *Jeopardy* dominance.

"I've got an idea to make this more fun," Jasmine said. "It'll give me a chance to play, too."

"What's that?"

"Wait until the Daily Double."

Three clues later, a contestant found it. Drew correctly answered, "What is the Mediterranean Sea?"

Jasmine slipped off her sweatpants using only her legs and feet and revealed her tiny white work shorts. She stood up and kicked her sweats across the room. Her shorts said "Playoffs" in blue lettering across the butt.

"Certainly raises the stakes," Drew said. Who could he even talk to about this night? Certainly not Niki. He wouldn't have to. Jasmine would probably tell her herself.

A minute later, the other Daily Double hit in the category of Italian Opera.

"I'm not gonna have a clue about this one," Drew said.

"You know the rules," she said. Next thing he knew, she was pulling his shirt off. "Are you cold?"

"Kind of," he said, but he was shivering more from nerves.

"Okay, babe. I'll share."

Next her sweatshirt came off, but instead of putting it on him, she wrapped it around his back and pulled herself closer. She was just wearing a tank top now.

"I'm guessing you worked a day shift earlier?" Drew asked as they leaned awkwardly and he computed the couch's dimensions in his head. He pulled off his shoes and started to lie down.

"Oh, a cuddler," she said. She finished her last drop of wine and set the empty glass on the floor by Drew's beer.

"If you lie down, will you behave?" he asked. Maybe the wine would cause her to doze off.

She nodded and whispered, "I like being told what to do."

Just like that, she was the baby spoon in his arms. He mumbled the last few Jeopardy answers with his arms wrapped around her.

"This is … pleasant," he said.

"Tell me what you want, and it's yours," she said.

He kept his chest back so his heartrate didn't scare her like the incident with Niki. He glanced down the couch at her legs. The tail of a dragon crept out of her shorts. A hypothetical conversation sprang into his head: *"It's just a tattoo, Mom. A lot of women have them."*

The commercial break before Final Jeopardy felt like an hour. Had the wine—or his company—lulled her to sleep? The clue appeared and the jingle began.

"It's the only letter in the alphabet not used in the spelling of any of the fifty states."

"What is Q?" Drew whispered. As the three-day champion's total was announced, Jasmine O'Keeffe turned without warning and slipped her tongue into his mouth.

Drew hesitated because all he could think about was how Jasmine O'Keeffe was only the second girl he'd kissed. Soon he got over the feeling of betraying Kelly.

The noises Jasmine's tongue made sounded louder than the music from the TV. Her kissing was far more aggressive than Kelly's. Yes, Jasmine was definitely a better kisser than Kelly.

Drew opened his eyes. Jasmine's were still closed. He paused long enough for her to notice. What if the kids came down? She wrestled him onto his back and climbed on top. Maybe the kids were used to this kind of thing from their roommate.

Jasmine let out a playful growl, raising her head and closing her eyes again as her hair flopped to one side.

"Do you want me?" Her voice was quite different, choking with lust. She bit the skin at the bottom of his neck. He didn't answer.

"Do you?" He nodded, but her eyes were still closed. She finally opened them. "Drew, do you want me?"

"I … maybe?"

She smacked both hands on his chest. "Wow, okay. Reject much?" She sat up and looked around, still straddling him.

"I told you I was bad at this."

"Don't tell me you're one of those guys who can't—" She grabbed his crotch and then raised her eyebrows. "Nope! That's not the problem."

"I'm single, but I still feel like I'm cheating on someone." He leaned up as a hint that she could dismount, but she didn't move.

"This isn't a date. I don't need dinner at Outback. Do you not understand what 'Come over and watch TV' means?" She playfully grinded her hips on him.

She added one more hip thrust. "You're the first guy to care more about TV than me."

"I don't care about TV. I still care about someone else."

"Who are you cheating on?" She grabbed his hands and put them on her thighs. Surprisingly, they felt more toned than Kelly's. He didn't let go.

"I said it just *felt* like cheating. It's not, but when you've got your heart set on someone else it just …"

"You and I sure handle things differently," she said, drumming her hands lightly on his chest.

"Yeah?"

"I'm getting over someone, too. This is how I cope. Rather than waiting and worrying, I move on. You should try it."

He let his hands slide on her smooth legs. "I've only been with one girl."

Jasmine laughed. "Oh, so that's it. You're a semi-virge." She grinded on him again and then stopped. "I shouldn't make fun of that. It's sweet."

Drew realized she wasn't going to dismount him during this heart-to-heart.

She put her hands on his shoulders, then slid them down to his biceps, which she squeezed. "I'd be crazy messed up too. She's beautiful." She was still gently rocking on him.

"She really is." He caught himself enjoying Jasmine more and more but didn't trust his control, so he tried to sit up again. She didn't budge, but she stopped moving. "Wait, you've met Kelly?"

"Kelly? Who is—Wait, is that who you're trying to get over?"

"To get back."

"Your ex-girlfriend's on your mind?"

"Most of the time. She's offered me a job, and—"

"This isn't about Niki?" Jasmine brought her hands back up to his shoulders and pinned him with her weight.

"C'mon. If Lee's dumbass can sense it, Niki definitely knows. Doesn't she?"

Drew stayed silent. He wasn't comfortable admitting it to himself, let alone Jasmine.

"For still having my pants on, I sure feel stripped and naked."

"I've been down that road, Drew. You can tell your brain one thing, but the heart wants who it wants. Corny as it sounds."

She looked at him, but he closed his eyes.

"Listen, sweet boy. You're going to have your heart broken, and you're going to break a lot of hearts. It's called your twenties. Speaking of, mine are almost over. Either way, if you're not honest with yourself, you're just wasting your time. Personally, it's not supposed to be this difficult when you meet the right person. So have fun in the meantime. Right?"

"I do know tonight is a long way from where I was five months ago. My Friday nights back then were mainly arranging my bourbon bottles in alphabetical order."

As Jasmine pressed her hands against her chest, Drew started thinking out loud.

"You said Lee can tell. I wonder if he's talked to Charlie."

"Oh, Charlie. He shot me down too. I mean, he was married at the time. Still, I wonder if he regrets it."

"I'm supposed to marry Kelly someday. I've known that since I was nine. My friends who met Kelly always understood."

"Does she know that? Is she acting like that's what's supposed to happen?"

Drew nodded.

"Do you think you were meant to only be with one person your whole life? God gave you this gorgeous body." She paused to tap his abs. "All so you could only share it with one woman?"

Drew closed his eyes and considered. Kelly didn't own him. Would it be wrong to have sex with someone else too?

"I never asked Kelly what her number of partners was. But she would always say, 'Be a mystery, not a history.'"

Jasmine leaned closer to his face and began to whisper.

"No one would ever know. I promise I'd make it so worth it." She kissed him again and then let out a long, soft moan. "All fucking night."

All Drew knew was that as soon as it ended—which would very soon if she continued her hips thrusts—he'd be flooded with regret.

"I can't," he said. "Even if I could, she would still find out. I'm not good at keeping secrets."

"Kelly or Niki?"

Another question he didn't answer.

Jasmine climbed off him. "You've got a lot to figure out, my friend." She began putting her sweatshirt back on, then sat back down to put on her sweatpants. "And I thought I was dysfunctional."

"Can you still keep this just between us?" Drew asked as he put on his shirt. "I'm clearly kinda messed up over it all."

Jasmine sat next to him again. She touched her hand against his jawline, almost motherly. "Darling, I'll do anything you ask. I wish nothing but the best. You'll figure it out."

"Sorry you had to cover Lee's tab for the bet you two had," Drew said.

She smiled. "What bet?"

19

"Ten serving nine," Bull called before smacking a hard serve towards Drew.

The pickleball took an odd hop and Drew barely returned it. Bull rushed to smash the game-winner at Drew's feet but aimed too low and put the ball into the net. Side out.

Drew took the ball and prepared his serve. Bull breathed heavily, and the front of his shirt was soaked in sweat. Drew took a deep, calming breath before adjusting his aim. Straight and deep would be safe. After his pre-serve routine, he fired a low bouncing shot that barely landed in. Bull couldn't adjust and awkwardly struck the ball out of bounds.

"Ten all," Drew said. As if cued by a stage director, Kelly entered. Was she timing these appearances on purpose? He turned back toward the court without saying hello. Instead, he lined up his next serve. A pickleball win must be by two points, so it was far from over. Both men went all out, each gaining an advantage and then losing it. Finally, Drew had the serve and a 14-13 lead for game point. Kelly spectating didn't matter anymore.

The point began with both players going conservative. Drew moved forward after hitting a shot to Bull's backhand. Bull struck it clean, so Drew had to reach as far as he could to return the ball with a grunt. It sailed past Bull and caught the outside part of the line. It was Bull's call.

"Out!" he said.

Drew deflated.

Kelly walked up. "Bullshit, Bull. It caught the line."

"I think we have bias situation here."

"Toward my ex-boyfriend?" She gave him a charming look.

"I thought you two are married." Bull smiled, shrugged, and walked toward the net. "Good game, Drew."

Stunned, Drew jogged up and tapped paddles, victorious over Bull for the first time ever.

"I get even tomorrow," Bull said before walking off the court.

Drew finally let himself take in Kelly's presence. She wore tight black shorts and a hot pink top, as if she needed more attention.

"See?" Kelly said. "You still need me." She folded her arms, extenuating her cleavage.

Drew grinned. "Thanks. I thought it was in too."

"Oh, I thought it might have been out, actually," she said.

It was in, Drew thought. He'd won without her help.

They started to walk toward the main gym together at a "let's talk" pace, like they were barefoot on a beach.

"That whole mortgage business my dad and his partners were considering? It's a done deal." She was giddy, but it felt staged.

Drew didn't reciprocate the excitement. "What happens next?"

They arrived at the workout area, and Drew realized that all the gym rats were staring at them. The overly buff dude who wore giant headphones. The middle-aged man who was always on the treadmill by the wall. Even the old lady who stank of cheap perfume watched them.

That's right, everyone. Drew thought. She's still mine.

"We meet with my dad. Not this weekend, he's on his way to Naples. Probably the following Saturday."

"I think I'm available," Drew said as sweat dripped off his chin.

"I should hope. What else would you have? You're not playing doubles with anyone else."

"I could ask Bull to join me on the men's circuit."

"Funny. How's our video doing?"

"I stopped checking." Would she believe that? "Over two hundred thousand views, probably."

"Maybe we should make another." Kelly smiled and raised her eyebrows. "The only question is if we're riding together or separately. Let me know next week."

"I will."

"What happened to your neck? It's all red, like something bit you."

I shouldn't have worn a tank top, he thought. "A spider. Big sucker."

"Gross. You really have to get out of that pit."

She turned and walked toward the ladies locker room, looking back once with a devilish smile. "Let me know about the ride."

Drew knew Kelly never drove to her childhood home and back without spending the night. It was more than an olive branch.

It was an invitation.

***

Drew sat at his desk, aware of Craig hawking him from his office all morning. His head still spun from the talk with Kelly when a customer entered the branch and asked for Drew by name.

At first, he thought the man was a mystery shopper. Corporate sent them to Craig every so often, maybe it was his turn. Instead of a hello, the stranger opened with a mighty handshake.

"My name is Brock Thorton, and I want the same loan rate you gave my cousin for his boat."

"I can certainly try, Mr. Thorton. How much are we talking about?"

"It's a hundred and forty-eight and four hundred ninety-nine smackeroos. I talked them down from a hundred and sixty. Can you believe it?"

They sat, and Drew smiled across his desk. "I'm going to save you even more money, unless you're not competing with your cousin." Drew had learned of a new policy since the last boat loan.

"Go on, my man. I drove two hours," Brock said from the edge of his seat.

"Set up an automatic payment from a new checking account here, and I can knock off a half-percent from the interest rate."

Brock whipped out his phone and punched in the formula to reveal his savings. A second, mightier handshake ensued, and Drew's knuckles popped. Over Brock's shoulder, Drew watched Craig step out of his office to mosey over to the teller line.

"You didn't do that for Jay?" Brock asked.

"Wasn't available then," Drew said. "They just came out with this deal, thinking it would be mostly for car loans under thirty thousand, but the savings extend to you, too. So as long as your credit's good," Drew said.

"How's eight-oh-five?" Brock gave a proud smile.

Drew entered the rest of Brock's loan application into the computer while the prospective boat owner played on his phone. Another customer entered the bank, a regular with too much time on her hands and her best years behind her. A pain, but she always enjoyed Drew's help with balancing her checkbook.

Craig knew her too, so he busied himself in his office while the lady stood a short distance from Drew's desk, jumbo purse in hand.

Drew paused his typing and turned. "I'm going to be a bit, Miss Morgan. Maybe you'd like our head banker to assist you today?"

He caught an annoyed glare from Craig, but Miss Morgan was sold on the title of "head banker." She entered his office before he could consider turning her away.

Drew carried on with the loan, the whole time wondering if he had the balls to put it under his number again. Drew overheard his boss's patience disappearing with each pointless question the old lady asked.

Was it better to let Craig finish first so Drew wouldn't have to decide? Drew couldn't risk hurrying the process and making a mistake on the loan, especially under his own number.

Craig rid himself of Miss Morgan long before Drew handed Brock his cashier's check. Another handshake squashed Drew's hand.

"Congratulations, on your new boat," Drew said as he wondered how a man could be so happy about owing so much money.

Only one task remained: entering a sales number. He knew what Kelly wanted him to do. He looked up at her banner and then at his screen. It waited for the three-digit code for the loan's creator. If Craig fired him, he would have no choice but to work for Terry Treader the rest of his life. The ring still waited for Kelly's finger, and with a job under her father, he'd earn enough income to marry her.

If he put it in Craig's name, perhaps his boss would forgive him for his earlier deed. Craig would treat Drew like a friend again, or at least not an enemy. The choice to work for Terry wouldn't be forced.

He looked over and saw Craig staring back at him. "Ball is in your court," he seemed to be thinking.

Yet Craig had nothing to do with this loan. Drew figured if he got fired, he could aim all of his heart to Kelly. They'd enjoy a short vacation and then move back in together and prepare for happily ever after.

He typed his number, 815, but something kept him from hitting enter. It meant telling Niki goodbye. It meant he would never live with Charlie. They might not even become friends, because it would continue a connection with Niki, and Kelly wouldn't stand for that.

He looked at the looming banner: "Let Kelly Treader help you land the home of your dreams."

He looked back at Craig. "Enough suspense, Drew. Who are you putting the loan under?"

"Me."

Click.

Craig let out a snort and left his door open to make the phone call.

"Yes, Frederick Adams, please. Tell him it's Craig." He spoke loudly and locked eyes with Drew. The small wrinkles on his forehead thickened.

Drew's mouth went dry. He looked up at the banner for comfort, but found none.

Craig kicked his feet up on his desk. "Fred! How goes it? We need to discuss a major attitude problem I'm having with my customer service associate who thinks he's a banker."

Craig's smile was over-the-top. "Andrew Brennan. The young guy."

Craig gave a proud smile, like he solved a Rubik's Cube for the first time, and looked over at Drew before mouthing, "That's you."

Drew did not break eye contact.

"You'd rather discuss in person? Perfect."

The stare down continued until Craig got up and shut his door.

***

Drew did not feel like going home at five. He was eager to exit the branch, but his decision to intentionally disobey his boss left him off balance. If given a redo, he wasn't sure if he'd make the same choice.

He knew Niki was scheduled to work, so Lee was probably sprawled on the couch like Jabba the Hutt after an all-you-can-eat seafood buffet. He considered texting Kelly to explain what happened with Craig, but if she knew he was desperate for the new job, he'd lose any control in mending the relationship. She'd manipulate him until he crawled back on his knees.

He needed to escape his own head. Find a place free from Craig, Kelly and even Niki. After digging through his wallet, he found the business card of Mikalis Andino. "Ulysses" was the name of the restaurant he owned. His phone's GPS told him the drive wasn't too far out of the way.

Drew arrived at a nearly empty restaurant and loosened his necktie. An older man sat at the other end of the bar and acknowledged Drew with a nod.

A sturdy bartender who seemed more interested in the smudge on a glass than his customers asked, "What can I get you?"

"Is Mikalis here?"

Establishing that he knew the owner earned Drew eye contact.

"Not for a few hours."

Drew scanned the steps of liquor bottles. Four Roses Single Barrel, Eagle Rare, Blanton's, and one near-empty bottle of Van Winkle lined the upper levels. At the top right, on a shelf by itself, sat his bottle of Devil's Rare 18. It had been opened, but only a dram or two had been drawn so far.

"How much for a finger of the bottle up top?"

"You don't want to know."

"I'm actually the one who sold it to Mikalis."

The bartender gave Drew a confused look, as if he'd ordered one of those non-alcoholic beers. "He must've given you a house for it. Four hundred clams an ounce."

Drew sat up straight. He tried to calculate how much of a profit Mikalis would make. Then he thought about the ring. Neither item would've done him any good. He should've kept the cash.

"An old-fashioned then."

"Sazerac okay?"

Drew nodded. Sazerac wasn't exactly a random house rye. How much was this going to cost him, three days of groceries? His phone vibrated, but he reached into his pocket to reject the call. This was going to be his evening and no one else was allowed to disturb him.

The cocktail was delivered in a fine crystal glass and looked so perfect Drew tried to sneak a snapshot of it.

"I consider my work art, too," the bartender said. Drew smiled and relaxed. He looked around for someone to toast, but even the old-timer at the end of the bar was on his phone.

A few sips in, a well-dressed older couple approached the bar but elected for a booth. Someday, Drew thought. How many decades had that couple been together? The gentleman wore a suit and the lady a dress, their wardrobes as dated as their skin. They were someone's grandparents who had probably been married so long they could read each other's minds. His drink sweetened with each sip.

"What would you like to eat?" the bartender asked.

"Thinking about it. Still unsure of dinner plans."

Drew skimmed the menu, fighting the temptation to splurge. A hint of loneliness crept its way in with an urge to take out his phone. But this wasn't a time to interact with Kelly or Niki. He ached to tell someone about the loan, for someone to be proud of him. He wanted to tell his father, but the man didn't do texting.

The list prices for the steaks could cover his groceries for a week, but then again, maybe his salary with Kelly in the upcoming months would make a temporary poverty mean nothing.

"New York Strip, medium rare."

I will have a date with myself. I will not worry about impressing anyone. Today's loan is my occasion to celebrate. Whatever happens, my life is about to change, whether it is progress or not.

Drew felt a vibration in his pocket. Maybe a phone call from his mother. She'd be proud of him.

His phone buzzed again, but shorter, signaling a text.

Drew's phone stayed in his pocket as the bartender brought out a basket of bread. If it was Niki he could invite her to join him, but what would be the point? She'd bring Lee and he'd embarrass Drew by ordering filet mignon well done with ketchup. It was time to evict Niki from his heart.

The steak looked beautiful when it arrived with perfect grill marks. Drew caught himself eating too quickly instead of savoring it.

"Another round?" the bartender asked with the Sazerac in his hand.

Drew decided another drink would corrupt his willpower.

"No, thanks. I just need to chill for a while."

The bartender dropped the check in front of him. "No hurry."

Drew lifted the piece of paper. If he took the job with Kelly, he wouldn't have to fret over prices ever again. He recalled how whenever they dined out, Kelly carelessly ordered appetizers that were clearly a rip-off. One birthday, he dropped almost two hundred on dinner for two. He ate hot dogs and ramen for a week and a half to compensate.

His phone continued its relenting vibrations. Drew dropped his napkin on top of the gristle and paid his tab. Finally, he pulled out his phone. The calls were from his mother. What was so urgent?

There were two texts from Niki. Both read, "Hey." Why twice? Did she wonder if the first one didn't go through? She rarely texted, so it had to be something important. Or she talked to Jasmine.

Three texts were from Kelly.

"LOL, Did you piss Craig off again?"

"We should talk."

"Let me know about the drive."

He decided not to reply to any of them. It was time to take control back from Niki and Kelly. His mother was a different story. Drew weighed his choices: call her on his way home or risk another pop-in visit. He dialed at a stoplight. Instead of a hello, she let her son know she'd heard of the developments with Kelly.

"Do you need help moving your stuff back in? Maybe it would be easier if I was there. Your father would help too. I heard Terry invited you both up for the weekend! Should I go too? I won't mention the waitress or anything, we can focus on your new job."

"Nothing has been decided, Mom."

"What are you waiting for? You can't risk letting her get away again."

The light turned green. "First, I really like my job now. I'm good at it, and I think I'm ready for a promotion." He left out the part about possibly being fired.

His mother sighed. "Is there a spot open?" Drew didn't answer. "That's what I thought. Even as a banker, are you really going to make as much as you would with Kelly?"

"My current boss makes enough to own a house and raise two kids with his wife."

"What's his wife do?"

"She's a teacher."

"She had to work six weeks after she had her kids."

"What does this have to do with me?"

"You know exactly what I'm getting at."

"The Treaders have enough money that if Kelly has to take maternity leave we won't miss any meals." He heard a sniffle on the other end of the phone. "Mom, are you crying?"

"I'm just so happy your heart is finally in the right place."

How did he get to discussing maternity leave? When the call began he had made no decisions. Still, his mother was pleased with him for once, just from a hypothetical. He knew how his father would feel, too.

He heard her blow nose. "Your grandmother. That's all she ever wanted was for you to marry Kelly. That's why she gave you her ring."

Drew didn't bring up the fact that he had to super-size the ring by selling his grandpa's prized bourbon bottle. He remembered the final time he saw his grandma. Her voice was scratchy and she had only days to live. "Andrew, I want you to have this," she sputtered through her pneumonia. "Kelly is the one for you. I can tell."

He took the box from his grandma and cried. This happened over a year ago, but it felt so recent. He didn't tell Kelly about it, because he wanted to surprise her when he was ready. Plus, he knew she would need more than an antique one-carat ring. That relic remained at his parents' house in his childhood dresser.

"Mom, I have to go. Traffic is crazy, and I need some time to think about everything."

She let out a deep sigh, one of her post-cry resets. "Okay, Andrew." Her voice was calm again, like when he was a boy and she was guiding him through a fight with friends. "I'm sure it hurt when Kelly said no. I don't understand it, either. But Terry implied to us she's been a mess. You two need each other. If you can forgive and not point fingers, it'll be worth a lifetime of happiness. And I meant to tell you ..."

More sobs.

"Your father wanted to know if you two would come visit while you're up here next time. I think he really misses Kelly."

"Of course that's who he misses," Drew said. "He knows he can just call her."

"I told him about your success at the bank. He sounded pleased."

"Awesome. I'm an only child and not even my father's favorite kid."

"You can thank me for getting you out of this mess at some point."

"I'll talk with Terry next weekend," Drew promised.

She sobbed again as they said their goodbyes while Drew parked at his apartment.

Niki's car was in the spot next to where he pulled into.

20

"There you are," Niki said. She walked down the steps in white sweatpants that sat low on her hips. The television blared the theme to *Wild Africa*. Niki sat on her usual side of the couch.

Drew held his phone out. "Sorry, I just saw your text on my way in." He crossed between her and a pride of lions on the screen. He didn't mean to sound terse, but he did feel like one more drink.

He pulled down one of his finer bottles, an Elijah Craig Toasted Barrel. Lee apparently helped himself to a bit of this one as well, Drew noticed. He could watch TV and wait for the bum to arrive, or he could take the bottle to his bedroom and continue his game of bourbon solitaire. The latter sounded better. He was about to pour when Niki came into the kitchen. He glanced at the impossibly low waistline of her sweats.

"I called off work tonight so we could hang out." She turned to head back to the couch, her Venus holes staring back at Drew.

He took a large swig straight from the bottle. A cardinal sin to serious bourbon drinkers. He placed it back in the cupboard and joined Niki on the couch.

"You talked with Charlie quite a bit the other night," she said.

The bourbon paraded down his throat. "Sounds like he's looking forward to coming home."

"It's cool you two are buds."

"We have a lot in common."

"He didn't respond to my email tonight," she said.

"Maybe he's just busy," Drew said and wondered if she needed consoling. "Hard to imagine what a soldier's life is like."

Niki shrugged, her eyes glued to the activities of the lions. The roommates sat together in silence listening to the British narrator describe the daily habits of the pride. It was almost dark outside, draining the light from the living room.

She'll fall asleep any minute, Drew thought. She didn't. Instead, another half-hour of nature entertained them both. Drew continued to sneak glances, but she remained wide awake. He returned to the kitchen for some water but ended up taking another swig from his bottle. This would give her time to curl up in her little ball and play possum so he could sneak upstairs and leave her alone. Let her experience rejection. Just because Lee was late didn't mean he'd happily fill in as second-string. How many nights had she been with her boyfriend while Drew isolated himself in his room? Niki needed to meet this new version of Drew who wasn't going to be a doormat.

A new show began about cave creatures, and it was so dull he was sure it would lull her to sleep. It didn't. Instead, Niki rose from the couch without even acknowledging Drew and walked slowly to the stairs. He watched her silhouette in the dark then shifted his gaze to her ascension up the steps where the dim hallway light shined. Near the top, her left hand, in one fluid motion, pulled the drawstring of her sweats. They loosened and dropped almost instantly. It happened so quickly, but with such grace, that he wondered if he'd imagined it. He wanted to chase up the steps after her like one of the prowling animals from their show.

He stood up, dizzy, but a different type of dizzy than what drinking produced. His entire body, shell-shocked with lust, begged him to follow her. He steadied his legs and reached the bottom of the steps. He listened to hear if the familiar rumble of Lee's truck was around the corner.

Nothing.

He picked up the remote from the couch and clicked the television off, but then turned it back on. Maybe she would come back down pretending nothing had happened.

But she didn't return.

By the first few steps, Drew was convinced that he had indeed imagined what he saw. The rest of her leg. A tiny hip decorated in pink lace. But when he reached the top of the steps, there lay the evidence: white sweats, as if her body vaporized and the clothing succumbed to gravity. A step into the hallway confirmed her intentions more: her shirt and the pink undergarments he'd only touched once when she forgot to take her clothes out of the dryer. He took a deep breath and stared at the trail of clothing in front of her bedroom.

The door was closed, except for a small crack. A sliver of light shone through, and Drew could tell by the way it danced it was from her candles. He gritted his teeth. He could enter and have whatever he wanted at the cost of betraying Kelly and Lee. It even felt like an act against his father. Or, he could start a new relationship that felt like it had been in progress since the day he moved in. All he had to do was push the door open. No words were needed.

She wanted him. He wanted her, emotionally and physically.

But he'd never be able to hide it from Kelly. Niki would break up with Lee, who would figure things out and tell Kelly, and everything Drew had suffered through would be for nothing. There would be no chance of working with Kelly, and Craig would find a way to fire him for the loans he'd claimed.

He would have to stake his whole future on what Niki felt for him.

Candlelight continued to dance behind the door, its orange warmth so inviting. It had been so long since he'd felt genuine affection. Kissing Jasmine was a mistake. What would sex be like with someone new? His body started to tremble, and he wondered if he could control himself. Which was the right decision? He would regret either course the next day, but he didn't want to make a choice he would regret the rest of his life.

He took two steps toward his own room. He passed her door and gave one more look at the path where her clothes led. She was not his to manipulate. What would she think when she realized he'd denied her? It could be a powerful feeling, and she might want him even more.

Drew quietly continued to his room, hoping she believed he was still downstairs. He opened his door and kept the lights off. He removed his pants and shirt, leaving them on the floor by his usual clutter before stepping carefully to his bed. A thin strip of light sneaked between his curtain to the pillow.

Her bare shoulder was the first thing he saw. Then an arm raised to guide him closer.

"There you are," she whispered. He heard himself inhale, almost like the beginning of a sneeze. "Just let this happen."

He did.

21

With Niki in his arms, Drew slept deeper than he ever had.

When he awoke, it surprised him that she had slipped away at some point during the night. Probably a precaution in case Lee dropped in.

When Drew sat up, his first thought was the void of any regret. This was better than any night with Kelly. Somehow their connection embodied long-time lovers, and the entire experience seemed to repeat itself like an echo throughout his body. He didn't want to leave his bed. Maybe she would return. Perhaps they could discuss how to rid her of Lee while minimizing drama. They'd figure out what to tell Charlie later.

As Drew showered and dressed, he still felt her body against his. He remembered her sounds, remembered her smell. The way she guided his mouth all over her skin. The taste of her tongue. The way they took turns gaining and losing control. The way she lay pressed upon him afterwards, exhaling and somehow weightless while his thumb stroked her lower back. Her skin was softer than anything he'd ever felt.

And now he was supposed to focus for another workday in the office?

The image in the bathroom mirror smiled back at him until he proclaimed out loud, "I love her." It was a relief that the rest of the world had to accept. His parents, Lee, and Kelly. Niki was his and he'd known it all along. Thank God he hadn't slept with Jasmine or anyone else.

Kelly was history. He didn't need Kelly and her lifestyle to be happy. He was in love with someone else. Whatever challenges were ahead were worth the price of that night and many more like it. Life without Niki was no longer an option.

Drew practically floated into his seat at his desk. Craig did a double take when Drew smiled at him. June's warm air flooded the lobby, and the branch stayed busy on a Friday.

Craig looked out his office toward Drew, like he wanted to tell him something. Then a customer would approach one of them, and it was back to busy work.

A late-morning lull gave Craig an opening.

"Before you take your lunch, I wanted to tell you Adams is visiting two weeks from today. To make it easier, you're free to put in your two-week notice. If I were you, I'd start getting my resume tuned-up. The two-week notice will prevent you from having the job termination on your record. I'll even put in a good word as a reference.

The condescension didn't shock Drew, it was the way Craig was so matter-of-fact. Drew gave no response, but he immediately began to question his night with Niki. How could he work for Kelly while he was in love with someone else? He now knew he couldn't forfeit this job so easily.

In the past when he was upset, he would take his lunch to Kelly's office. But that morning, the thought of her made the guilt bubble up in his stomach. He needed to find out if she could sense he was in love with someone else.

He told himself he'd done nothing wrong because he and Kelly weren't together anymore. His heart made its choice: Niki Benson. A relief spread through his body, and his heart was healing. At eleven thirty he grabbed his lunch and took the elevator to the third floor.

With each cubicle he passed, someone would turn away and then look back. At first he was amused, but what did they know?

It all made sense when he arrived at Kelly's office. The calendar, photos, and personal items were gone. Only the desk and file cabinets remained. The only trace of Kelly ever working there was part of a word that hadn't been erased from her whiteboard.

Humiliated and blushing, Drew sulked back to the elevator.

"She thought she left one of her jackets," he said to anyone listening. Then he realized he was still carrying his lunch.

A scary idea crossed his mind. Had she been fired because they knew she was leaving? Could that happen to him?

Drew tried not to panic, but when the elevator opened back on the ground floor, Craig was waiting with arms folded.

"Oh, did someone not tell you she resigned? Sounds like you two lovebirds are really patching things up. Maybe this time around you just won't communicate at all, huh? That way there's nothing to fight about."

Craig's sarcasm ignited something within Drew. He took a step closer to his boss.

"What is your problem with me?" Drew didn't care who heard.

Craig took a step back as Drew continued.

"I've done everything around here for weeks while you pretended to visit dealerships. You act like I torpedoed your career because of two loans. Just because your personal life is miserable doesn't mean you need to take it out on me!"

Craig smiled like a boxer who had been struck with a sharp jab to the chin. "Oh Drew. I could ruin your little world so easily." He shook his head. "I'll be out at the dealerships all afternoon."

He started toward the exit. "And take Kelly's banner down by the end of the day. Do what you want with it."

Drew returned to his desk, the old pit of anxiety pulsing in his stomach, and he couldn't face the thought of lunch. He wasn't sure telling Craig off was the right decision, but it made him feel better. Maybe that trend was getting him into trouble.

As quitting time approached, Drew could only think of Niki. She was supposed to break up with Lee today. Knowing Lee, he'd shrug it off and move onto someone else. Maybe even Jasmine O'Keeffe. Thank God he said no to her. Niki wouldn't have touched him after that. Now he had to cleanse his pallet of Kelly, and what better way than to tear down an eight-foot banner that never blinked.

After the lobby doors were locked, Drew carried a chair over and scanned the beautiful face that controlled him for so long.

"Need help?" one of the tellers asked.

Drew ignored the offer and stood on the chair. His hands shook. Only a thumbtack held each corner. They didn't come out of the wall easily, and a thin layer of dust coated the banner. When it finally flopped to the floor, he felt victorious but confused.

One teller applauded. It's possible someone comprehended the monumental significance of what he'd just forced himself to do.

Kelly's face stared up at him from the floor. "Home of your dreams" it still beckoned.

"I'm taking this to the dumpster unless somebody wants it."

"She'll probably want it," someone else said. "You should take it to her."

With a twinge of shame, Drew rolled it up and stuffed it into his trunk. Maybe he and Niki could use it as a bonfire to snuggle up to some night.

On the drive home, Drew's feelings sorted themselves out. It felt odd hauling Kelly's banner in his trunk. But it was only a banner, he reasoned, not a dead hooker.

He knew Niki was scheduled to work, but he was ready to stay up late on a Friday to connect with her again. His spirits lifted the more he thought about it.

Niki was the right decision. Niki was the right decision.

Everything would turn out how it should. If Kelly couldn't bother to tell him she'd resigned, that answered the question as to if she was serious about their future together.

"Oops," Drew said as he sped through a light that turned red. There was no hurry, unless of course Niki called off work. The possibility thrilled him. After all, her friends would understand after a breakup. Jasmine would call her a "lucky bitch" and tell her how obvious it was that Drew was in love with her.

As Drew wondered how Lee would take it, he realized he never overheard them having sex.

"Hello!" Drew said as he pulled into a parking spot. Niki's car was still there. She must have called off, and Lee's truck wasn't around. It would be a night off for

Drew and Niki. An encore. Kelly would always interrupt their quiet evenings by taking work phone calls.

His heart raced as he sucked on a mint. He'd just go in and jump her. They didn't need to talk until afterward. He would carry her right up the steps and into her room. She'd been just as bold less than twenty-four hours ago, now it was his turn to express how much he wanted her.

He counted to ten, his body tense with anticipation, and then walked to the front door. When he opened it, Niki was behind it on the floor, hugging her knees and sobbing. She turned, and it reminded Drew of the first night he saw her when Charlie was moving out.

Her eyes were puffy and her makeup left small dark streaks under each eye. She wore her tiny blue work shorts and a white nylon top he hadn't seen before. It left the small of her back and her arms bare.

"What did he do to you?" Drew said, striding toward her. When he knelt, his tie almost gagged him.

Niki kept sobbing. Her phone was next to her, and she couldn't get any words out.

"Did he hurt you?" Drew hadn't thrown anything approaching a real punch at someone since third grade, but he was ready to hunt down Lee wherever he was.

"Ch-Charlie," she finally whimpered. "He's dead."

She buried her face in his chest. As the information sank in, Drew felt ashamed. Her brother had died, and he found himself relishing the touch of a grieving sister.

"I didn't get to say—"

Drew hushed her and let her cry as he adjusted his legs to sit next to her more comfortably.

He rubbed her back. "He knew you loved him. He talked about you every time we ..." It didn't stop her from convulsing. "Shh-shh-shh," was all he could say.

They stayed like this until the sun shifted enough to darken the room. His legs cramped and his back ached from their awkward embrace on the floor, but he wasn't going to let go of her. She was his to look out for now.

"He loved you very much," Drew whispered. "I'll take care of you now."

He loved her too, but it wasn't the time to tell her. He figured Charlie would be happy to know Drew was with her.

The room grew darker and Drew's body ached everywhere. A familiar rumble crept up from outside. Drew prayed it was someone else with an obnoxiously loud vehicle, but he knew better. Lee took three attempts to get the door unlocked with his key. He entered, bringing his usual cloud of leftover cigarette smoke with him without closing the door all the way.

He stepped over Drew's extended legs and pulled Niki from the embrace without a word. He carried her up the steps like a sleeping baby while Drew sat stunned and empty. His shirt was damp and stained with Niki's tears. Drew rose, and closed the front door.

His back and legs were stiff with pain, but not as much as his heart.

At some point that night while Drew slept, they disappeared. He wouldn't see either of them the rest of the weekend.

Niki never called or texted back, so Drew tried Lee. On Monday during lunch, Lee finally sent back a message.

"just a small family thing"

It took Drew more than two hours to gather the courage to respond.

"Charlie was my friend too."

Drew felt he deserved the chance to mourn him no matter where it happened. He clicked around online and only found mention of a future service to be held in Pittsburgh at a date to be announced once the body was transported home. Cause of death: friendly fire.

Drew didn't tell anyone at work about losing his friend. Craig didn't know anything about Charlie, and Drew worried it would make him sound like he was playing the sympathy card. He had no urge to mention it to Kelly, wherever she was. It was time to cut ties from her as soon as Niki returned, whether Drew had a job or no job.

Niki couldn't stay sad forever, and he'd do everything he could to brighten her life. They could watch animal shows or go out to dinner, and he would even take her back to that dance club if she wanted. Drew contemplated calling his mother and telling her that she'd just have to accept his new girlfriend, who wouldn't be a bar waitress forever.

At night he lay on the couch and fantasized what a life with her would be like. For every concern his conscience spewed, he reflected back to their night together. Could that feeling really be his for the rest of his life? He'd do anything to make it so.

On Tuesday, Drew texted her.

"I miss you."

She didn't reply, but when Drew got home Lee's truck was double-parked in their lot. The thought of Niki spending another night with Lee made him sick.

Drew parked and turned off the engine. At that moment in the silence, the severity hit him. Charlie was dead. He'd never get to meet him in person. They were supposed to live together, and now they would never shake hands.

Like an avalanche, the finality struck him, and he found himself clinging to the steering wheel and crying. *How had I held this back for so many days?*

He was more worried about Niki than her dead brother, but he made a vow. "I'm sorry, buddy. I promise I'll take care of her the rest of my life," he repeated over and over.

Drew wiped his face and looked at his glazed red eyes in the rearview mirror until he thought, *So what?* They needed to know he was crying.

He ran his hands through his hair, making it messier. Dark circles hung under his eyes. He hadn't slept well since Charlie died, but if he was honest with himself, it was more about Niki being gone. Especially the way Lee took her away from him.

He imagined Charlie advising him, "Tell Lee to hit the road. Tell Craig there's no way you deserve to be fired from your job."

Drew gathered himself for another few heartbeats before slowly walking to his front door. He paused before opening, like he needed permission.

When he entered the living room, the smell of Mexican food struck his nose. They must have gotten takeout without him. Maybe Lee would actually take his leftovers home instead of leaving them in their fridge for a month this time.

What he found were Lee and Niki in the kitchen, cooking together.

A Creed song blared from a phone on the counter, and he could hear laughter from both of them.

"Drew!" Niki called in happy surprise. "Just in time for dinner."

Lee drained the last of his can of Budweiser and squashed it between his fingers.

"You want hard or soft? The taco shells I mean. Don't confuse me with Jasmine." He laughed then belched.

"I'm not hungry," Drew said as he tried to make sense of the scene. "Why didn't anyone ..."

They didn't hear him. Lee fed Niki a sample from a wooden spoon.

"I gotta get domesticated," she said as she held her hand up to her face.

"What?"

She leaned her back into Lee, who put an arm around her, "I gotta get domesticated." She wiggled her fingers.

Drew tilted his head. Had she put his ring back on? No, what she was showing off was much smaller.

"Christ, Drew," Lee said. "We got engaged!"

Niki pointed at her pebble that was barely a carat, and it certainly didn't sparkle. She held her smile like someone patiently posing in a group selfie.

He stared at her hand as Lee pulled her tightly against him.

"That's what you … You're marrying him?" Drew asked.

Lee shook his head as though he pitied that Drew couldn't understand. "We're trying to have a positive day since the last few have been such bummers." Lee pulled out a chair. "Have a seat and come party with us. Beer?"

He pecked Niki on the cheek. "Only happy thoughts today," they said in unison.

Drew turned. "I just can't," he said and retreated to his room.

He changed out of his work clothes with all the enthusiasm of a zombie. Disbelief enveloped his sadness.

He ignored the growls from his stomach as he lay in bed. His mouth was dry, and all he could feel was a hollow heartbeat.

The apartment didn't feel like home anymore. A move was inevitable. Certainly Lee would push for the transition, unless Niki would let him continue to loiter rent-free.

Exhausted, he laughed at himself for feeling comatose in bed while the sun still shined through his blinds. The joyful noises spewing from downstairs did not help him relax. He tensed his angry body and shut his eyes until his muscles grew tired.

He wasn't sure if he was awake or dreaming when a moment of clarity struck. *There is no longer anyone else I have to worry about making happy.*

He reflected on these days while Niki was AWOL. He didn't concern himself about what he wore. There was no laundry left in the dryer, nor did Lee flop his ass on the couch. To go that many days without a whiff of cigarette smoke made looking for his own place sound so much better. He only needed the means to afford it, so still having his job by Friday at five would certainly help.

Drew became alert and unable to zone out. Overhearing Lee say stupid shit from downstairs was going to drive him mad. He threw on some dark jeans and a wrinkled polo shirt.

He tried to sneak out of the apartment, but Niki spotted him and made sure he wasn't unacknowledged.

"Where you going, roomie?"

"You haven't called me that in weeks."

"We're getting spicy in here," she said as she finished the last of a taco.

"I just need to ... not be here," he said. He caught a glimpse of a disappointed look on her face.

"What did you expect?" he said as he turned away.

He drove straight to Ulysses, betting he could rediscover the positive vibe from his last visit. While approaching the door, he realized he was underdressed. Older couples in business attire excused themselves past him as he U-turned. He retreated to his car and observed them through the windshield.

Some walked ahead of their partner. One couple held hands. Another pair were each on their phones as the host opened the door for them. When was it going to be his turn?

On a whim, he checked his pickleball video.

The number of views: More than two hundred and fourteen thousand.

The top-liked comment: "These 2 go to the same gym as me, and I can tell you the hot one broke up with him. LOL"

As the evening sun lowered behind a storm cloud, he started his car again. He circled past the bank because he didn't know where else to drive until he aimed himself on the familiar route to Kelly's condo. He deserved an explanation of her abrupt resignation.

He pulled into a gas station to fill up and typed out a text. "I'm coming over." However, he didn't hit send because Charlie's theory came to mind. If she was cheating, maybe he could catch her and the other guy together.

He drove by Kelly's place twice before parking in his old spot. He wondered why he found himself rooting to catch someone. Maybe it was his guilt from sleeping with someone else. He would have to keep that from Kelly for the rest of his life.

He caught himself recalling his night with Niki again as he unbuckled his seatbelt. If nothing else, at least he knew what it was like to have sex with someone else. The jury was still out on whether Kelly was dull or Niki was that much more amazing. Anything was better than loneliness, he told himself.

He got out of his car, determined to put Niki behind him. She was a nymph waitress who stole his heart for a few months and made him realize how miserable it was to be a third wheel.

Drew approached Kelly's front door. It would feel weird to ring the doorbell at a place he used to live. He gave the door three solid knocks with his middle knuckle. As he waited, his mind drifted back to Niki showing off her sad excuse for a diamond ring. He was about to knock again when the door opened. It was Kelly in yoga pants and a black sports bra.

"Sorry to pop in like this. Did you just get back from the gym?"

"No, I bought some cardio equipment and put it in the spare bedroom."

"And that's why you haven't been to the gym much."

"I didn't know you were playing detective. Come in and have a post-workout drink with me."

She led him to the kitchen table where they'd eaten countless meals together. By habit, Drew took the chair furthest away.

"Have you seen my lucky cup?" Drew asked. "The purple one."

Instead of answering, Kelly laughed. "That's not why you're here, is it?"

"I had to ask something stupid. Lee is not fun to share conversations with. Or the same living space."

Kelly poured a glass of white wine. Forgetting he was a guest, Drew opened the refrigerator himself. Their prom photo remained near the top.

"Wait, you have beer in here?" Two green bottles sat next to the orange juice.

"Leftovers from my dad. You can take them."

"Heineken? I could see Terry liking these for some reason." It had been awhile since Drew had cracked open the trademark green bottle with the red star on the lid.

"Dad loves his imports. We met the other day so he could update me on the new job."

Drew tried to twist the cap off. "You left the bank without telling me. Why?"

Kelly looked away, twisting her glass by the stem. "You're going to need a bottle opener. Let me find one." While she dug through a utensil drawer, she explained herself.

"I absolutely had to get out of there. I was stressing myself out, and I had to stop taking on new mortgages. Obviously, I planned on leaving anyway, so why start with new clients, right? Closed my last few and that was that. I burnt my vacation days and brought all my crap home."

Kelly found the opener and presented it to Drew.

"Don't you get bonuses for leftover vacation days?"

"That's only a banker thing."

Drew popped the lid off and watched the tiny cloud of vapor rise from the open mouth.

"I'm sure dad will be more than fair with our time off." She smiled.

"That's a bold implication. But it might be my only choice, pending my meeting with Craig. I'm glad I can trust you if you want me to lose that job so much."

"Is it still that bad?"

"Craig is trying to steal the bonuses I earned from two gigantic boat loans I logged under my code."

"I swear, he is obsessed with his bonuses," she said. "I was so surprised he actually took a vacation with his wife. Hope it was worth it."

"I'm interested to hear your entire lowdown on Craig now that you don't work with him anymore."

"Is he back to being happily married?" She took a longer sip, and Drew wondered if she wanted him to stay and get drunk with her.

"Who knows. I meet with him and Adams next Friday to try and save my job."

"Just quit ahead of time."

"Can't. One, I need the paycheck. Plus, I want to beat Craig at something. He's been such a dick to me. I don't even know what I—"

Drew felt himself choking up. The emotion was an abrupt mass he was unaware he carried.

Kelly scooted her chair closer and rubbed his back. "I get it. That place can be toxic."

"It's not even that place. I actually like it there. It's ... him!"

His voice cracked. He stopped talking, reluctant he might cry.

Kelly took both his hands. "Listen. I can help you get out of there. Hell, you can quit tomorrow. Who cares, right?"

Drew looked up. There was a sparkle of emotion in Kelly's eyes. She tilted her head. "I knew there was a drive in you. You've proven it. That's all I was looking for. Do you get that now? Do you understand why things had to be like this?"

He nodded. "But it was another thing to admit it." He grabbed her hands tighter. "Any ideas on how to beat Craig?"

Kelly released his hands, "Men!" she screamed and leaned back. The kitchen turned so silent Drew could hear that the fridge kicked off. He looked around, noting how everything in Kelly's home was so much better than his apartment dwelling. Matching steel appliances of the latest models, better lighting, not a trace of cigarette smoke. If he asked, would she give him his key back?

Kelly sighed. "Craig is obviously using company time for whatever he wants. Adams might not even care as long as the dealership loans keep rolling in." She looked upwards like she was trying to remember a detail. "To his credit, those car loans are his doing."

"Two against one. I'm screwed."

"Those two aren't as tight as you'd think," Kelly said. "Adams fired a banker for refunding too many fees for a customer. He can be heartless and takes his bottom line very seriously. I guess that isn't exactly the greatest news for you."

"But the boat loans were mine. I don't see the big deal."

"Craig has an ego. He's territorial. Trust me, if he refers a client to me, he makes sure he gets his credit. So when he trained you …"

"I trained myself!"

"He gave you an opportunity, though."

"But it almost feels personal. Like he hates me."

"You purposely disobeyed him. The first time, he might have forgiven you." She squinted. "The second one, I think you're the one who made it personal. Like I said, ego. Sure, he's friendly in the branch with customers around, but I've seen it at meetings behind closed doors."

"Throw in the issues he's having with his wife, too."

Kelly shifted in her chair. "There are certain people who let their pride wreck them. Are you sure you can't just quit?"

Drew shook his head and finished his beer. A small buzz warmed him. The image of Niki and her ring still stung. He doubted he could handle going home without running into their further celebrations. The last thing he needed to hear was the two of them fucking each other's brains out.

Kelly backed her chair away from the table. "I'm planning on going to bed soon."

Drew stood up. "I should get going then. I'll figure out what to say by next Friday. Tell me if you think of anything else."

Kelly laughed.

"What's so funny?"

"I guess we're driving separately to my dad's house then." She mashed her lips into a forced smile.

He knew she was inviting him upstairs. If he spent the night, that would show Niki.

Something felt off about accepting the offer. Kelly wasn't who he wanted. He weighed the prospect of sex with his ex-girlfriend and learned that Niki owned his heart. He knew if they went through with it that much like last time he'd be thinking of Niki's body, especially now that he'd experienced it.

A burp slipped out the side of Drew's mouth, and Kelly slightly recoiled.

"Well, off ya go," she said. "It's a school night, and I'm all sweaty. You're being sent home, mister."

"Some decisions are harder than others," he said.

"I'll meet you at my dad's home at noon, okay?"

Drew nodded, but he didn't want to leave. She hugged him and made her "mmm" sound, which meant, "I appreciate the affection, but it's over as soon as this hug ends."

"See you Saturday," Drew said. "Thanks for the Heiney."

***

Drew awoke Saturday morning, refreshed but unsure. He remembered a dream from his slumber. In it, he walked to a college class wearing what felt like a weighted backpack. Anytime he removed a strap, the other strap would slip back onto the opposite shoulder. He couldn't get the backpack off no matter how hard he tried. He wondered if the backpack represented Niki or Kelly. Perhaps it stood for something intangible, like his job, his mother's hopes, or his father's approval.

He pondered the dream as he headed downstairs. It was impossible to pass the top few steps without thinking about the way Niki undressed on them. He replayed that moment a thousand times. Then there she was on the couch.

"I didn't know you were up," he said.

"Lee had to head out early for some branch emergency involving plumbing." She laughed, but Drew didn't reciprocate. She curled her legs in front of her, the diamond ring resting against her calf.

"Glad you won't have to borrow my ring anymore."

"That's the closest you've come to telling me congratulations."

"How did you think I'd feel?" He stopped in front of her, staring down. "You both ghosted me."

"You're really raising your voice to me after I lost my brother?"

Her face dropped behind her folded arms, and a sob escaped.

"He was my friend too," Drew said with a softer voice. "I'm sure there's a reason you're engaged to Lee, even after the agreement we—"

She stopped crying and lifted her face. Her soft, brown eyes captured him. "You would ruin me."

"I would've done anything for you." Revealing this was cathartic.

"That's what I mean. You would absolutely ruin me." Her face dropped briefly, then she looked back at him with fresh tears. "The way you loved me would ... I'm just not ready for that."

"You were ready enough to invite me into just about every other part of your life."

"I'm twenty-one. I'm not ready to fall in lo—"

"*You're engaged!*" His voice echoed through their entire home.

"Lee will never set a date," she answered calmly. "He just wants to take care of me because Charlie's gone."

Drew walked to the kitchen and started his coffee. "I'll be moving out soon I guess." It was easier to say that from a different room.

"You don't have to."

Drew let that statement hang for a long time as he watched his coffee finish. He couldn't decide if he wanted to make her feel guilty or rotten. He could easily say many things that would burn the bridge to Charlie's sister forever.

With one of Charlie's old camouflage travel mugs in hand, he returned to the living room. "I'm doing my best to fall out of love with you."

Niki covered her face again. Drew returned upstairs and packed a bag to spend the night at the Treader house. Right or wrong, it would help his healing process.

Niki hadn't moved when he came back down. She was still crying. He wanted to comfort her in his arms and convince her to end it with Lee, but he realized she was right. There was no way she was ready for him. He would never hold her again.

He stood by the door, ready to leave her.

Niki looked up. "Please don't go." Her beautiful brown eyes were puffy.

If the meeting with Kelly and her father went well, then it would only be a matter of time before he moved out.

"There's someone else who's ready for me," Drew said.

Niki nodded and curled up into a ball. Drew set down his coffee and his bag, then walked over. She was now silent, and he kissed her on the temple.

As he walked out the door, he heard her sobs begin anew.

22

The longer the drive wore on, the more Drew grew anxious.

His last conversation with Terry was the humiliating, yet accurate, discussion about proposing. *"Sir, you were right at that moment, but since then I've grown in my work ethic and commitment to my future with Kelly,"* was a conversation icebreaker he rehearsed a dozen times in several variations until he arrived in the driveway and was greeted by that man.

"Welcome Drew. Good to see you again. We're in the parlor."

The Treader family's glorified living room without a television was for some reason referred to as the parlor. Drew recalled his mother fawning about it on a drive home when he was a teenager. "I can't believe we're friends with people who have a parlor!" she would say.

"Our house barely has room for TV trays, they have a parlor."

Drew took a seat on one of the parlor's three antique couches. Kelly sauntered in wearing a yellow summer dress that hugged her upper body but floated over her legs. Her bare feet gave off the impression of some young temptress lured in from a flower garden. Her entrance felt orchestrated.

Terry was busy at his bourbon station. "What do you feel like today? I've got some Booker's."

"I don't think I've seen a bottle of that in the wild since the Cubs' last playoff appearance," Drew said as he happily accepted.

He poured two, but left Drew's pour much shyer than his.

"Rocks?" Terry offered. Drew slowly shook his head as he compared the serving sizes.

"Dad, don't short him just because it's your good stuff," Kelly said as she finished scrolling through her phone.

Terry frowned. "He can have more if he wants. I want everyone in their sound mind while we discuss business."

He sat next to his daughter on the antique couch that was from France. "Kelly told me she's discussed her professional future with you."

Drew nodded and sipped half his pour.

"I hear you're doing better at the bank, even though the position is minor. Would you be interested in learning the mortgage business?"

Drew nodded again.

Kelly laughed. "Drew, you're allowed to talk. Jesus, Dad, do you have to be so formal?"

Drew shot her a thankful smile. "I'm interested. I wouldn't be here otherwise."

Terry closed his eyes for his next statement. "I know you two have had your differences. For this partnership to work, you'll need to resolve those."

"We're working on that," Kelly said. "Aren't we, Drew?"

He hated the way she made that sound, but he stood his ground. "We are and will continue to."

"I don't know if I'm convinced. I can't invest in someone who's going to break my daughter's heart."

Now Kelly was giving him her father's same cold stare.

"I'm finding that I'm hitting a ceiling at the bank," Drew said, each word feeling more awkward than the last. "There's nothing I'd like more than to advance my position professionally."

"Tell him about the business itself," Kelly said. "No, wait, I'll do it."

Terry gestured that the floor was hers.

Kelly and her cleavage leaned in. "There's a growing demographic of young people in the Chicago area moving to the suburbs." Her voice turned to the professional tone he overheard on so many business calls, but now he saw how much she waved her hands as she spoke. "College grads with old money making new money. The housing market is booming because of it."

"That's why we're putting you kids into the equation," Terry interrupted. His hands stayed folded. "We need young people who can relate and have the energy Kelly brought to that rinky-dink branch. We'll also handle any other mortgages, but our marketing will aim at first-time homeowners."

"I follow," Drew said. He was tempted to add, *This sounds like a great idea if there's no bullshit,* but he kept that thought to himself. He knew there was still too much to learn before they would consider him at their level.

"I'm prepared to offer you a base salary of ninety-five thousand."

Drew nodded poker-faced while his heart screamed, *That would do it!*

"Kelly, of course, will have a salary as well. I'll let her decide about its confidentiality, but I'll expect the best from you both. You follow through with that, the sky's the limit. It could even become your company someday, young man."

Drew shifted and finished his bourbon. He could treat himself to two steaks and three old-fashioneds every week on that budget. Probably splurge on a pour of the Devil's Rare 18 with his Christmas bonus. "What's the timeframe for all this?"

"We're estimating a few months, say the beginning of September. It's best you continue your role at the bank until mid-August, but Kelly needed to depart sooner for obvious reasons."

"To be honest, her getting out of Dodge still isn't obvious to me."

Terry turned sharply toward his daughter. "Does he not know about the situation?"

Kelly worked fast to shut this down. "It was nothing, Drew. Office politics. It was easier for me to disappear."

As Drew struggled to make that sink in, Terry smiled and raised his glass. Drew tentatively raised his empty one, but couldn't bring himself to grin.

"Let me know when you have an answer." Terry stood and gave Drew a pat on the shoulder. "I'll leave you two alone," he said as he refilled his glass and left the room.

"What do you think?" Kelly said excitedly as her father's footsteps faded away.

Drew considered his own father's feelings. As much as he didn't want to admit it, his parents' opinion still weighed on him. "I know I can do this job. I'm wondering about us. How do we start fresh?"

"We both said and did things we regret," she said. "I'm committed to forgiveness."

Drew felt the tension clear out of his head now that Terry was gone. "What should we do about our living arrangements?"

"I think it's kinda fun living apart for now. Going to your place that night was like ..." She tilted her head until she found the right connection. "It felt like college. Remember when all we did was have sex at each other's apartments?"

"Fondly."

"Once the job begins, it would make sense to live together by this fall. It's not like you have any important stuff to haul around."

Drew's mouth twisted. Wouldn't it be great revenge to have Kelly at the apartment any night she wanted? She could make sure every one of her orgasms rattled the walls of Niki's bedroom.

Kelly stood up. "I don't want that to influence your decision on this, so dad and I both agree you need to think about it at least a few more days."

Kelly walked over and sat next to Drew, her leg leaning against his dress pants.

"Good idea," Drew said. He knew his heart wasn't ready to accept her back quite yet either. He'd have to somehow purge Niki from both his mind and heart. "I better head home soon."

"Not yet," Kelly said. "You drove all this way up here. We can talk more about the company, or let me know if you think of more questions for Dad."

"I didn't know you had any situations at Midwest. Everyone there worshiped you."

Kelly shook her head. A strand of hair hung over her nose, and Drew brushed it back behind her ear.

"Most did. You know how that goes. Once you're on top, people want to bring you down." She smiled. "And I like being on top."

Oh, what the hell, Drew thought. He leaned in, and they began kissing like teenagers who'd hidden under the bleachers of their high school.

"Again …" She pecked him on the mouth.

"I don't want to influence …" Another peck.

"Your decision." She scooted back and now it felt like those same teenagers had been sent to Bible camp.

Drew realized he'd lost control. Kelly was back to dictating the levels of affection.

"Do you want another drink?" she asked as a way to keep the mood light.

Drew's overnight bag was in his car in case this turned into a visit of booze. If he spent the night, at least he had a change of clothes for his walk of shame when he departed.

"I don't think your old man wants me to drain his good stuff."

"Dad?" Kelly called out. "Can we get another round of the fancy stuff?"

She must be the only person who he'll take orders from, Drew thought. Terry popped his head back in the room.

"Actually, I'd be fine with something lighter," Drew said. "Maybe a beer?"

"Any preference?"

"Got any Heinekens?"

Terry frowned. "Heineken? I haven't drunk that tap water in years. It's always skunky. I'll pick one you'll like." Terry disappeared again.

Drew looked at Kelly. Her cheeks were scarlet.

Drew almost bit through his lower lip. He let out a small laugh with what little wind was left inside. Charlie was right. Everything made sense. She had been with someone else, it didn't work out, and now Drew was her backup plan.

"I have a lot to think about," Drew said. He exited what he sometimes imagined was his dream house without saying goodbye to anyone.

23

The anxiety of waiting for Friday's encounter with Adams skyrocketed after Drew's epiphany with Kelly.

There were so many unanswered questions: When did her rebound romance start, how long did it last, how long had his beer been in the fridge. Would he even want to know the answers?

Maybe it had to do with why she left the bank so suddenly. She mentioned "office politics," and that could have meant one of her co-workers found out about it. Drew was kicking himself for not forming any kind of an alliance with the tellers. They probably all knew her secret and enjoyed keeping it from him.

Drew was overwhelmed by the possibilities as he entered the branch Monday morning. Craig gave him a good morning wave with a sarcastic smile.

When Drew sat down, the first thing he noticed was the void of Kelly's poster. It was still in his trunk. He'd forgotten to hand over the souvenir before his abrupt departure.

Calm down, he told himself. Be ready to fight for this job. This week he would check loan retention to see if Craig's plan was worth all the risky loans for the bank. He needed to somehow identify which dealerships Craig's loans actually came from. If they were all funneled in from one or two dealerships, what was Craig doing with all that other time?

He knew he could plead to Adams that he felt he warranted the bonuses because those loans were linked to a military friend who was killed in action. If Craig called bullshit, Drew could bring Lee in to verify. Drew could also demonstrate his value to the company was that he allowed Craig to earn new business without being in the branch. Drew knew he had solid strategies on his side.

His thoughts shifted to Kelly and whether he overreacted. He was just as guilty of trying to move on with someone else. The difference was that Kelly could have told him when her affair was over, and she didn't. He believed she was so handcuffed by guilt that she didn't even chase after him.

One conflict at a time, Drew decided. He would go back through each closed loan and count each dealership that the cashier checks were addressed to. Or he could search upstairs where they kept all the vehicle titles and total them that way. A plan and the answers would come, and he was certain he would be as prepared as defense attorney at a murder trial.

Several customers kept him busy the first part of the morning. As he finished with a woman who needed a new debit card, he didn't notice who walked into the branch.

"Fred! How goes it? Your short game any better?" Craig's voice sent Drew into a panic.

He looked up and saw Regional Vice President Frederick Adams in the lobby chatting with Craig. Drew didn't remember the last thing he said to his customer, but as soon as she was gone he walked over to the people who would decide his fate.

Craig grinned. "Did I say he was coming Friday? Oops. I meant today," he said as he headed toward his office. "Won't you join us?"

Drew's legs wobbled as he entered. Adams sat in Craig's chair. He was a shorter, much older man. His stiff stature made it look like he had something to prove at all times.

"Andrew Brennan, is it?" Frederick Adams' voice was aged, but friendly. Drew nodded and settled next to Craig where the customers normally sat.

"Mr. Devlinger tells me you two are having a dispute. Maybe I can settle it quickly, because I'm not thrilled with having to drive all the way over here."

Drew reminded himself to breathe. Adams didn't feel all that threatening, but shouldn't they have shaken hands? He took a deep breath and spoke.

"Mr. Adams, I just want you to hear my side."

"Cute," Craig said, exchanging a glance with their moderator. "I trained you to do loans. You're not a banker yet, so you don't get to dip into my bonuses." Craig held up a thin stack of papers then double-tapped them on his desk. "Long story short, I helped you and you took advantage."

"My turn?" Drew asked. His adrenaline pumped as he struggled to steady his voice. Adams nodded, and Drew began.

"I've been doing all of the work while Craig is barely in the office. I'd like to know how many dealerships are actually sending us these loans." He glared at Craig, who looked away. Drew knew he was onto something. "While I'm closing loans and opening accounts, you're off at Wrigley Field."

Craig choked out a laugh. "Can I tell him? No, you do it."

Adams adjusted himself in the chair. "There are instances when, yes, I reward some of the area bankers with tickets, but only after Mr. Devlinger assured me he'd been at the dealerships after work hours every night."

Craig chimed in. "Drew, I believe you once benefited from hockey tickets because Kelly was too busy to use them."

Drew began to feel hope fade. These two golfed together, dined together, and hell, probably had Niki serve them at Playoffs a time or two. He'd have to swallow his pride and forgive Kelly. He squirmed in his seat trying to alter his strategy. That's when he remembered what Kelly told him about Craig's ego.

"Is what I did a fireable offense?" His voice finally firmed up. "Certainly, I've—"

"The first time? No," Craig said. The smirks were gone from the room. "The second time while I was here after we'd already discussed it? Definitely. You don't even get bonuses in your role. It's not in your contract. I would've gladly bought you another gift to show appreciation."

Adams raised his eyebrows.

"Ah, the gift card." Drew pulled out his wallet and slapped the plastic down on the desk. "Twenty-five bucks to The Cheesecake Factory. Reminds me of last year's Christmas party when we all received …" Drew paused. "Oh! Twenty-five bucks to The Cheesecake Factory."

Craig and Adams exchanged a glance as Drew put the card and his wallet back. "Don't worry, I still have my other one. The closest location shut down right after New Year's."

Drew realized how loud his voice was, and that he sounded unprofessional or ungrateful.

"We don't solve problems at this bank with rants," Adams said icily.

"Do you know where that bonus money goes now, Drew?" Craig's tone was extremely condescending. "It goes to nobody. Happy? Let's see how much you actually cost me."

He slid the sheets over so hard they spilled into Drew's lap.

Drew fumbled and flipped through the paperwork, trying to make sense of the columns and rows. The report was dated for the past three months, so he could measure a good bulk of his work. The boat loans would have added another quarter-million in total loan numbers. No wonder Craig was so upset.

There was a category for accounts, deposits, and average sales per new customer as well as ranking. Craig was first in the company in almost everything. What Drew saw on the last page didn't register at first. It was a six hundred and fifty dollar bonus for perfect attendance.

Sick days taken: Zero.

Vacation days taken: Zero.

One time in his college dorm, Drew was playing poker with the older guys. He wasn't dealt many good hands and was ready to push his stack all in just so he could spend his night doing anything else. Then he was dealt quad nines. Four of a kind out of nowhere. The memory danced in his mind.

"This is for April, May, and part of June, correct?" Drew's voice quivered, but now from excitement and confidence. Adams learned forward, so Drew held the sheets out for him to inspect until he nodded.

"I still don't know why Mr. Devlinger should get credit for the loans when he wasn't in the branch," Drew said.

"Because I networked those loans through the dealerships." Craig was so loud the tellers probably heard him.

"Not the boat loan."

"I would have closed that loan, but I was on vacation out of the country!"

Drew thought back to the poker table's reaction when he slammed down the four nines. "Odd," he said. "Because you didn't bother to tell the bank you were on vacation. Have you spent the six hundred and fifty dollar attendance bonus yet?"

Adams' wrinkles appeared against his eyebrows. "That better not be the case," he said as he reached for the report.

Craig's face turned beet-red. "That's not a big—"

"This is company fraud, Devlinger!" Adams tossed the sheets at him. To Drew, it was a ticker-tape parade.

"A week with his wife," Drew said. "I take it you didn't get a postcard, Mr. Adams."

Craig's eyes became enraged. He stood up and yanked off his jacket.

Adams shook his head and stood up as well. "This is grounds for almost certain termination."

Craig didn't acknowledge the statement. He glared at Drew, and for a moment Drew wondered if he was about to absorb a punch to the nose.

"That was the week Kelly changed her mind and wanted you back, wasn't it?" Craig stared down at Drew. "You idiot. She didn't go back because she was sorry. She used you to get even with me."

"Jesus Christ, Craig," Adams said. "You cheated on Sarah?"

Drew's insides plummeted. The Heinekens. The strange hours. If true, it would hurt worse than any punch. How could he ever touch Kelly again?

Adams walked from behind the desk and began explaining the termination process and something about Drew taking over, but it didn't matter.

"Guess I should clean out my desk," Craig said. He was so deliberate and smug for some reason. He opened his bottom drawer and pulled out Drew's lucky Northwestern cup.

"Want this back? I gotta go."

24

The manager of Windy City Jewelers sat across from Drew in a back office. The smaller room lacked the soap opera lighting that flooded the sales floor, where everything felt like part of a dream sequence.

"I'm sorry, Mr. Brennan. Our return policy is sixty days. You're a few weeks past a full refund."

"Sir, it's the same diamond as it was a few weeks ago. Do you not understand how hard this is on me? As a man, can you imagine how my life has been since she said no?"

"I just wish you would've returned it then," he said. Drew noticed this older man didn't wear a wedding band and wondered if it was because he had been burnt too.

"How much can I get for it?" Despite Drew's promotion and considerable raise at the bank, there were still thousands on the line.

"I can give you two-thirds of the cost. I wish I could consider negotiations, but our corporate policy was in all the sheets you signed when you purchased the ring."

Drew thought about all of the fine print on the loans he closed every day. No one read much of anything. They simply trusted the company was fair. Trust wasn't something he had a lot of anymore, and he realized he'd overlooked so many important details about Kelly.

"Basically, I just rented a ring for a few months," Drew said with a sad laugh. He thought of the night when Niki got it stuck on her finger.

The manager smiled. "You can always hold onto it and try your luck down the road."

"Don't you think it's bad mojo to put a ring on a woman after another one turned it down?"

"That old expression: 'What they don't know …'"

Drew smiled now. The offer on the sellback would be more than enough to cover the security deposit and two months of rent on the new apartment he hoped to move into by the first of July.

"I guess I have no choice but to accept the two-thirds." Drew started to stand.

"There's one other option, Mr. Brennan. I normally don't do this."

Drew sat back down.

"You can get a full refund for one hundred percent store credit, so when the right person comes along you'll already have it paid for. Who knows, perhaps by then you'll be ready for something even more spectacular."

Someone else? The hypothetical didn't even sound appealing. Last Thursday he treated himself to another old-fashioned at Ulysses. The previous Sunday he attended a Cubs game without talking to another soul there. He'd beaten Bull in pickleball their past two attempts. Solo celebrations were his new bag.

"I'm fine with two-thirds. I need the money more than I need a wife." He laughed, letting the manager know the negotiation was over and he could laugh too.

The next morning, Drew's savings account was higher than it had ever been.

25

It had been months since Drew's last visit to his parents' home. He remembered snow on the ground that weekend, during life before the breakup.

His mother pleaded with him for days to visit for Fourth of July. The bank was closed for the holiday, so he agreed to spend the afternoon relaxing with her.

When he pulled up to his childhood home, Kelly's red MINI was already parked.

Kelly waited, staring through the screen door, her hair as blonde as it was in their prom photo. Everything about her was still breathtaking, but after the surprise of seeing her came the pain. She was on his turf now. When his mother found out the truth—and he would hold nothing back—she would realize what he already had: Kelly would never be the one.

"Surprise," Kelly said, opening the door. "I understand why we haven't spoken in forever, but I missed you."

"There are only the pursued, the pursuing, the busy, and the tired."

"Huh?"

"My favorite line in *The Great Gatsby*. Courtesy the one class in college where I remembered learning anything."

Drew saw his mother standing behind Kelly, and neither noticed his scowl as he gave her a hug.

"You didn't warn me we'd have visitors."

His mother didn't answer.

Drew heard a familiar creak of the floor. His father's footsteps from the bedroom to the living room sounded the same as they had when he was a small child.

Rick Brennan stood before his son. He appeared years older than when Drew last saw him.

"Hi," Drew said. He couldn't get past the deep wrinkles on his father's forehead and that his thin hair was now completely gray. "You doing okay?"

His father had always been shy, especially when feelings were involved. Perhaps his most apparent Irish trait. He looked away when he spoke.

"Andrew, it's not fair to avoid Kelly's calls. You two need to talk."

"Not if you have to trick me into doing it," Drew said.

His parents left the room, and Drew sat in his father's recliner, a dinosaur of a chair that would never be considered to exist in the Treader parlor. Kelly sat on the couch, her legs crossed in a baby-blue summer dress.

"This was the only way," Kelly said. "Please let me explain."

She touched her face. Here come the waterworks, Drew thought.

"I don't know what I was doing. I just felt lonely and angry."

She began to cry. Drew's expression didn't change.

"I made one mistake, Drew."

"How many times did you make that one mistake?" He knew his parents were listening.

"I wanted you to hurt as bad as I did for walking out on me. For giving up on us so easily." Her face was soaked in tears. "I didn't want you to move out, you know that. And then you shacked up with some tramp."

Drew didn't feel sorry for her. He thought back to those first lonely, awkward nights in a strange bedroom. He remembered how Craig treated him, and how Kelly only came over that night because Craig was gone with his wife. No wonder Craig wanted him to keep it a secret. No wonder Kelly told him about putting loans under his own number.

"Is Craig getting a divorce?" Drew asked.

Kelly frowned. "I don't know, and I don't care. I don't want anything to do with him ever again."

"Must suck to be his wife and kids right now."

"Are you just going to torture me with all the things I said I was sorry for?"

"The hockey tickets. That was a plan to get me out of the house that night."

"No! Nothing happened before you and I broke up. It was when I heard you were falling for your roommate."

"You probably believed everything Craig told you about me."

Kelly stopped crying, though her face was bright red. "Nothing happened with your roommate that whole time?"

"Lee's fiancée?" He hadn't lied yet.

"They're never getting married, and you know it."

"Craig sure keeps you updated."

"Answer my question, Drew. You had a thing with her, didn't you? Lee certainly thinks that you did."

That's when his father walked back in.

"This fighting needs to end. You two should've never broken up. Drew, it was your fault for moving out so quickly. What did you think was going to happen leaving a woman as beautiful as Kelly on her own? Was she going to wait around on you?"

Maryann held back tears as she tentatively entered and sat next to Kelly.

"Think about our families. Think about your grandparents," she said as she glared at her son. "A few months ago, you wanted to make Kelly your wife. Both of you need to swallow your pride and forgive. Nobody cheated on anybody."

He thought about telling them the truth about Niki. Maybe not the whole truth, but at least telling everyone that he experienced very strong feelings for her. That would hurt Kelly and piss off his parents even further.

Drew turned to Kelly. "For the rest of my life, my parents will side with you, since you're the one trying to repair the relationship." He took a deep breath and wished he had a beer. "What I'm saying is, it looks like a long shot that I'll be staying through dinner."

"Neither of you did anything that isn't repairable," his mother said in a softer tone. His father nodded.

"And the Cubs are only five games out of first in the Central. I suppose their playoff chances are repairable too."

Drew recognized that his life's turning point would unfold with whatever he said next.

"It would be so much easier to forgive you. But Craig had my cup."

"Your what?"

"My lucky purple Northwestern cup. When I moved, I searched and searched for it."

His mother scoffed. "Are you listening to yourself? Lucky cup! Grow up."

"He took the cup from our cupboard before I even moved out." Drew stood up, his stomach twisting at the revelation. "This began before I proposed."

Kelly lowered her chin.

Drew walked into the kitchen, dizzy. He pulled out the drawer that held the kitchen trash. The scent of coffee rinds and last night's pork chop scraps smacked him, and he lurched. From the other room, he heard his father tell Kelly she needed to leave.

***

On his drive home, Drew stopped at a gas station two blocks from the bank. It wasn't for a fill-up, it was to park next to its open dumpster. He popped his trunk and stared down at the banner. He picked it up, tempted to unroll it and gaze at Kelly's image one last time.

"Home of your dreams," he mumbled.

Drew jumped when he heard a disgusting cough from behind the dumpster. He then cautiously peered around the side.

A homely man stood up. "You getting rid of that?" he pointed at the banner Drew held clumsily to his chest. "I could use it."

"For what?" Drew asked.

"No holes in it, are there? I need a tarp."

Ashamed, Drew handed him the giant canvas.

"No holes. Just a pretty face and a bullshit dream."

"Got'ny change?"

Drew opened his wallet and pulled out two gift cards. "Ever been to The Cheesecake Factory? It just reopened."

The man accepted the two plastic cards like they were holy communion.

"Tell them Craig sent you," Drew said as he climbed back into his Civic.

At a stoplight on the drive home, he opened the YouTube app on his phone and deleted the pickleball video. It had garnered over a half-million views.

26

Drew spent a lazy September Sunday on his own couch in his own apartment. He'd gone to the Cubs game by himself the night before. In the midst of a six-game losing streak, the only highlight was Pearl Jam frontman and celebrity Cubs die-hard Eddie Vedder throwing out the first pitch.

That afternoon, he rested up for an evening pickleball session. It was a smaller, neighborhood event with only a few other singles who enjoyed playing under the lights of a converted tennis court. Bull would be there, but at best he only beat Drew one out of five attempts anymore.

Drew learned to be alone without loneliness. His banker salary provided a comfortable bachelor lifestyle, and though his apartment was tiny and ten minutes further from work, there was never pressure to be anywhere else. If he felt like a barstool and a beer, he headed a few blocks away. If he wanted to catch a Cubs game, he'd find a cheap ticket and stay as late as he felt, even on work nights. Banking became easier every week. It's no wonder Craig dominated the company numbers, the branch stayed busy merely from its convenient location.

His parents still spent time with Terry, but they knew better than to invite Drew to the usual functions. There was no mention of the Treader annual work picnic where he fell in love with Kelly as a child fifteen years before.

Drew had initiated a tradition with the tellers where he bought bagels for them every Friday, and as he predicted, it began paying dividends within a few weeks that they looped him in on their gossip. They told him Kelly was thriving at her father's new mortgage company. Good, he thought. But whenever his mind lingered on her too long, images of Craig quickly sent him into a disgusted state of regret.

Something interesting began happening to Drew. Other women approached him. Not necessarily as directly as Jasmine O'Keeffe, but a night at the bar often yielded a phone number and the occasional date. None of the women felt like a true connection, and one that he particularly fancied came clean with him after their second drink.

"You're still healing, aren't you?"

Drew nodded. He wasn't going to lie to himself anymore. Life was just beginning to belong to him.

It was on that Sunday afternoon when he received a text that shook him out of his comfort zone. It was Lee.

"What's ur address?"

He answered with the information promptly. "Am I getting a wedding invitation?" Drew added before hitting send.

Drew still thought of Niki, more often than Kelly. He drove by Playoffs and spotted her car only once. It was a moment of weakness after a lonely night, but he realized perhaps Niki's only purpose was to get him through those God-awful months. If he never saw her again, he knew she would always wonder 'what if?' as much as him.

Lee texted again. "R U home?"

Drew's temperature rose. "I am, but I have pickleball soon. What's up?"

Lee still hadn't responded by the time Drew was ready to leave, and he didn't like the idea of Lee hunting him down.

Drew planted his feet and threw practice punches at the thin air. His left jab made his elbow hurt.

There was a *Bang-bang-bang!* on his front door.

Drew took a deep breath for the showdown. When he opened the door, Lee was finishing a cigarette.

"Long time, no see," Lee said.

"They must have you fixing things at the other branches."

Lee dropped his smoldering butt and scraped his shoe over it. The smoke followed them in.

Drew couldn't read Lee at all. "Want a beer?"

"This won't take long," Lee said.

He couldn't remember Lee ever turning a beer down. When he sat, Drew relaxed a little. No one sat down to throw a punch at a guy.

"How are things? Niki good?"

Lee nodded.

"Set a date yet?"

"I always wondered about you two," Lee said. "I mean," he interrupted himself to laugh, "I could straight out feel your jealousy every time I came over. You were about as friendly as fire ants even before we got engaged." Lee scratched his ear. "I had a hunch."

"What does it matter?" Drew asked. "Did you two set a date or not?"

"We did not. Something came up," Lee said. "She's pregnant."

The last piece of Drew's heart that still clung to hope crumbled into his lungs. Maybe it was for the better. He'd let the maintenance man gloat if it meant he never had to see him again.

Lee suddenly cared about the Cubs highlights on the television. "They win today?"

"Lost nine to six. No chance they make the playoffs."

"Onto hockey, right?" Lee seemed happy again. His laugh wasn't sarcastic. Drew unclenched his fists and dropped his shoulders, but he wondered if his pal was toying with him.

"Maybe we can catch another game," Drew said before remembering that could have been the night Craig went into his bed and stole his lucky cup from their kitchen.

"I remember that night," Lee said. "Remember what we talked about?"

"Nothing too serious, was it?"

"Bless your heart." Lee sprung up from the couch and pulled out a box of cigarettes. He played with it in his hand. "You don't remember what I told you?"

Drew shook his head. "Were we upset about how much beers cost?"

"We talked about starting a family. You wanted one, I didn't."

"Sounds like me. The old me at least."

"I told you I got snipped."

Lee's smile covered his entire face. He bounced with a little exhaling laugh. Drew felt overheated again.

Lee leaned forward and slapped Drew on the back.

"She's out in my truck with her stuff. Says she's ready for you to take care of her now. Y'all can have each other."

Drew's mouth opened. Lee exited, closing the door only most of the way. Drew tried to stand, but his circulation didn't oblige. He sunk back into his couch.

Then he heard a meek knocking.

EPILOGUE

Four years later ...

An April morning smothered the Rosehill Cemetery with fog.

Two grandparents each held the hand of a small boy who was more interested in the footprints he left in the wet grass than the man buried six feet below.

He squeezed his grandma's hand. "When does hockey start?"

"Tonight. Your daddy wants you to take a long, long nap today after you play with Grandpa."

The boy bent down and wiped the damp grass. "Is Mommy coming too?"

"Just Daddy, once he's done training new people at the bank." Grandma exchanged a grin with Grandpa. "We can call Mommy after your nap," she said. "Maybe a video chat even."

"Why isn't Mommy coming?"

It was Grandpa's turn. "She'll be back tomorrow. You get to spend the day with us until then."

"Why?"

"Because of her new job. She has to help doctors get new medicines to help people."

The boy looked to the sky as a jet circled O'Hare. He returned his attention to the grass before stepping to the stone in front of him. It was a place he'd visited many times. He liked the angel on the stone and the American Flag next to it. Grandpa showed him how to salute.

They stood with their thoughts through their silent ritual until grandpa took the boy's hand.

"Time to go home. Are you ready to go get a bagel, Charlie?"

Acknowledgments

Thank you, readers. I worked very hard on this book, so if you enjoyed it, help me spread the word by leaving a review anywhere you can. It means the world to me that you took time out of your life to read my story.

Thank you to my wife, Beth, for the constant support and especially for listening to me for countless hours as I talked about this story so often. You continue to be my muse.

Thank you to my editor, Greg Hardy, for working so hard on helpful feedback, masterful revision and fine-tuning my prose. Your brilliance reflects throughout this story.

Thank you to Daniel Schmidt and John Ghirardi for their bourbon expertise.

Thank you to Vicky Constantinidis for her mortgage expertise.

Thank you to Stephanie Bleser, Sam Lyons, Justin Leuthauser, and Brittany Freeman for feedback on those earlier drafts when I was still figuring these characters out.

Thank you to all of my beta readers, especially those who went above and beyond to provide helpful feedback including, Sarah Smith, Patti Seidel, Jennifer Curtis, Thomas Penney, Joey Murray, Justin Wojtowicz, Rebecca Jaegers, and Kevin Kafoury.

And finally, my students. Thank you for listening to my tangents and ramblings. I hope you've graduated, otherwise our next chance at eye contact might be somewhat awkward. Either way, I'm glad you read.

ABOUT THE AUTHOR

Rob Durham is a high school English teacher, a stand-up comedian, and an author of several books including the highly praised *Don't Wear Shorts on Stage, Around the Block,* and *Don't Do Shots with Strangers.* An Ohio native, he moved to St. Louis in 2005 and married his wife Beth a few years later.

When he's not in the classroom, Rob enjoys pickleball, chess, and taking Ohio State football games way too seriously. You can find his comedy tour schedule on RobDurhamComedy.com and follow him on Facebook, Instagram, and TikTok @RobDurhamComedy.

Made in the USA
Monee, IL
26 February 2022

91887191R00142